notorious

it girl novels created by Cecily von Ziegesar:

It Girl
Notorious

If you like the it girl, you may also enjoy:

Bass Ackwards and Belly Up by Elizabeth Craft and Sarah Fain

Secrets of My Hollywood Life by Jen Calonita

Haters by Alisa Valdes-Rodriguez

notorious

an it girl novel

CREATED BY

CECILY VON ZIEGESAR

LITTLE, BROWN AND COMPANY

New York ❧ Boston

Little, Brown and Company

Hachette Book Group USA
1271 Avenue of the Americas, New York, NY 10020
Visit our Web site at www.lb-teens.com

First Edition: June 2006

Produced by Alloy Entertainment
151 West 26th Street, New York, NY 10001

ON THE COVER: dress—ABS by Allen Schwartz, earrings—H&M,
necklace—stylist's own

ISBN 0-31601186-X

10 9 8 7 6 5 4 3 2
CWO
Printed in the United States of America

With affection beaming in one eye, and calculation shining out of the other.

—Charles Dickens

A WAVERLY OWL IS ALWAYS POLITE,

EVEN TO TOTAL STRANGERS.

T insley Carmichael glanced back at the sparkling Hudson River. The roar of her family's orange seaplane lifting back into the azure sky announced her return to Waverly Academy, the exclusive upstate New York boarding school she'd been unceremoniously kicked out of last spring. The *pop-pop* of her pencil-thin heels on the steps of Dumbarton Hall reminded her of flashbulbs, and Tinsley felt her classmates' eyes on her, peering out of the dorm room windows above her head. She shook out her mane of long, purpley black hair and turned her head to give her fans her best side, anticipating their hungry questions: *Ohmigod, where have you been? How come you're back? Weren't you kicked out? Were you in rehab? Is it true you threatened to burn down Stansfield?* And finally: *How come Callie and Brett didn't get into any trouble and you did?*

Tinsley would simultaneously deny everything and fan the

flames of speculation. She'd especially enjoy encouraging the theory that she'd selflessly taken the rap for Callie and Brett after all three of them were caught on E last spring, the spring of their sophomore year. Her two best friends would be more than a little shocked to see her. She hadn't spoken to either of them over the long summer, and she still had no clue why *she* was the only one actually expelled for the whole "incident," unless one of them had ratted on her. But now that the summer was over—a *phenomenal* summer at that—and she'd been readmitted, she was feeling generous and willing to forgive and forget, as long as Callie and Brett provided the requisite profuse apologies and a healthy dose of ass-kissing.

With its pristine, ivy-covered brick buildings and undulating green playing fields, Waverly Academy looked like the ginger-bread-cookie version of Brown or Princeton. As Tinsley clicked her way down the hall to Dumbarton 303, she recognized the familiar smell of Callie's coconut-scented Bumble & Bumble detangler and Le Petit Prince baby perfume mixed with the stale stench of Parliament cigarettes. She smiled as she pictured what would happen next: she'd waltz into their triple dorm room and throw herself across her old bed just like she used to do after a long, boring lecture in Hunter Hall or Mr. Farnsworth's calc class. Callie's little pink mouth would drop open and she'd try to say something cool but choke on her words. Brett would be amazed and astonished and totally speechless. Then both girls would begin squealing like baby piglets, flinging their slender limbs around Tinsley's neck. Well, at least that's how she imagined it.

She flipped her white plastic aviators up on her head and

readjusted the bleached-leather hobo bag Chiedo had made for her while they were on safari outside of Cape Town. The memory of summer in South Africa made her chest ache—the parties at CapeRave with Chiedo and his friends, watching the sun rise over Table Mountain, and *Where I've Been I Would Not Go Back,* the heartfelt documentary about the people of South Africa that she and her father had made over the course of the summer. She touched her shark-tooth necklace (Chiedo again, sweet Chiedo), flipped her long, shiny dark hair behind her shoulders, and flung open the dorm room door. *Ta da!*

The silence she'd expected was of the stunned variety, not the where-the-fuck-is-everyone variety. But where the fuck *was* everyone? Tinsley surveyed the landscape: the view of the sparkling Hudson River through the wide casement windows, Brett's blue-and-white Nantucket beach etching sitting on her dresser, the litter of empty Diet Coke bottles on the floor next to Callie's bed, the ashtray full of Parliament butts on the windowsill. But no Callie and no Brett.

She wrinkled her nose, detecting a scent she didn't recognize— could it possibly be White Petals, a Chanel knockoff that stunk up Greenmarket Square in Cape Town? She sniffed, tracing the smell to a waterfall of unruly brown curls hanging off the side of her old bed. *There was a girl in her bed.* The girl shifted in her sleep. Tinsley kicked the antique-oak bed frame with her well-heeled foot. "Who are you?" she demanded.

"I'm Jenny." The girl sat up abruptly, her eyes darting wildly around the room as her ridiculously huge boobs bounced. "Who are you?"

Tinsley threw her bag down at the foot of the bed, her nose still wrinkled in distaste. Definitely White Petals. "Where are Callie and Brett?"

"They"—she started, rubbing her big brown eyes—"were here a minute ago. What time is it?"

"Time for you to get out of my bed," Tinsley announced coolly.

Jenny shook her head, trying to lift the sleepy haze from her brain. The stunning, tall girl standing in front of her was wearing a white-on-white leaf-print camisole and no bra. Jenny stared enviously at her browned shoulders and the outline of her round, perky breasts. What she wouldn't give to be able to wear a shirt like that. The girl had long black hair and impossibly blue—almost violet—eyes. . . . Wait a second, *her* bed?

"You're Tinsley!" she squealed a little too emphatically, bouncing up and down before remembering she was wearing the soft, super-thin white Constance T-shirt she liked to sleep in. She hoped her enormous breasts didn't look too ridiculous as they bobbed and settled back into place.

"I don't remember you." Tinsley folded her arms across her chest as if to imply that Jenny had better put her boobs away before she hurt someone with them.

"I'm new. I transferred from Constance Billard." Jenny pointed at the capital letters emblazoned across her T-shirt and then remembered her boobs again. "In New York City," she added hopefully, as if the fact that she was from the city would lend her an air of credibility or at the very least a remote hint of cool.

"I know where it is," Tinsley snapped as her white aviators

slipped down off her forehead, landing perfectly on the bridge of her tanned, pert little nose.

Jenny could feel her glaring intensely from behind her sunglasses. She'd worried about meeting Tinsley since Dean Marymount announced her return to Waverly last night. But now that she was here, Tinsley was even more intimidating than Jenny had imagined. And she was supposed to live with this girl?

"You mind?" Tinsley asked, opening her cool, beat-up-looking leather bag and pulling out a clove cigarette.

Jenny shook her head and offered up the Powerpuff Girl Zippo she'd bought in Chinatown that she used for lighting the apple cinnamon candle she kept by her bed. "Wake and bake, right?"

"It's not pot." Tinsley pushed her sunglasses up again. "So what year are you anyway?"

"Sophomore." Tinsley blew a smoke ring like the caterpillar in *Alice in Wonderland* and Jenny remembered what Sam, the boy on the train when she first came up from New York, said about Tinsley going to parties at Bard and the rumors she'd heard about Easy and Tinsley hooking up behind Callie's back last year. Jenny imagined boys drooling over Tinsley's smooth tanned shoulders and her wild violet eyes and girls hating her for the same reasons. Jenny would have hated her too if she didn't feel simultaneously scared and infatuated by her.

"So you're the new roommate, huh?" Tinsley examined Jenny as if she were a vintage fifties housedress from Goodwill that could either be an incredible find or, on closer inspection, just pit-stained and worthless.

"Yeah. Callie and Brett are awesome," she replied with a borderline squeak, hoping to let her new roommate know they were part of the same fold now. After all, she'd made friends easily with Callie and Brett. Well, sort of easily. Callie had kind of bribed her into letting the Disciplinary Committee believe Easy Walsh was caught in their room on the second night of school visiting her rather than Callie, his girlfriend. In the end Easy took all the blame, and part of Jenny thought maybe, just *maybe*, it had something to do with her.

She shot her feet out from under her scratchy baby-blue wool blanket and shuffled over to her antique oak bureau. She grabbed a bottle of Pantene de-frizzing serum and squirted a dollop into her palm. It made a little farting sound and Jenny muffled a squeal of discomfort. Then she turned to the mirror as she smoothed out her long brown tendrils, grateful that at least she didn't have any embarrassing morning whiteheads around her nostril creases.

"So—" She turned around, freshly de-frizzed.

But all she saw was the door closing. It slammed angrily, and Jenny couldn't help but jump back a step. Hello, that was not a real fart!

Outside the casement windows the first leaves were beginning to turn orange and red and the Hudson River rolled along, smooth and sparkling under the morning sun. A feeling of dread settled in Jenny's stomach. Was it just a bad first impression, or was the famous Tinsley Carmichael kind of . . . well . . . a *bitch*?

SageFrancis: She's baaaaaaack . . .

CelineColista: What r u talking about?

SageFrancis: TC! She's returned from exile in Africa or wherever the hell she was. I heard her father had to promise Waverly a new performing arts center to get back in.

CelineColista: No waaaaaaaay . . . Do you think they'll kick J out of 303?

SageFrancis: I heard they're ALL staying. Do you think she'll clash with T?

CelineColista: Who knows, but if they do, I want popcorn and a front-row seat!

A WAVERLY OWL KNOWS THAT FORGIVING IS NOT THE SAME AS FORGETTING.

Callie Vernon dragged the narrow heels of her new black-and-white Louboutin mules through the dewy grass toward Chapel, the fuzz of sleep still thick in her brain. It had been three days since the Black Saturday party, but she still couldn't shake the image of Jenny and Easy staring into each other's eyes by the reflecting pool at Heath's Woodstock estate. Was that even *true*? Heath had sent everyone a gossipy email after the party suggesting it, but she still didn't know for sure. Either way, the fact that Callie had set it up—she'd actually *asked* Easy and Jenny to flirt in order to make it look more realistic that Easy had been visiting Jenny and not her when he was caught in their room by their freaky dorm mistress Angelica Pardee—threatened to reduce her to a MAC-mascara-streaked mess. And if that wasn't enough, had she really gotten so drunk that she made out with Heath Ferro—gross!—*and* begged her old boyfriend Brandon to hook up with her? And had he *really* turned her down?

"That you, C.V.?"

Callie felt wobbly already, but when she spotted Tinsley in the chapel doorway, she was sure she'd lost her mind. She stopped and tilted her head to the side, expecting the violet-eyed heavenly apparition to float back into the atmosphere. Her old roommate's appearance at the top of the stone steps was as much a dream as Dean Marymount and Mrs. Pardee measuring room 303 for a fourth bed last night, their voices the unintelligible murmur of angels. Their announcement that Tinsley had been suspended and not expelled for their raucous night out on the playing field last spring was too fantastic to be true—yet here she was.

Callie wanted to run and jump into her arms. She wanted to explain to Tinsley about Easy and Jenny and the Disciplinary Committee and the distance between her and Brett and how Brett was secretly doing it with Mr. Dalton, the new theoretically doable history teacher, who was actually kind of gross to imagine Brett doing it with. Things had been so weird with Brett that she'd actually found out about Mr. Dalton by answering Brett's cell and talking to her sister. She'd pretended not to know until Brett told her about the affair last night, but she'd actually been the one to slip the secret and get the whole school talking about it. Oops. Now Tinsley, the only person Callie had ever met who could vanquish even the most serious problems with little more than a smoldering wink, was back. But a hazy corona settled around Callie's head, and all she could do was stare.

"Hello?" Tinsley demanded loudly, interrupting her daze.

Her voice sent Callie galloping up the chapel steps. She wrapped her arms around her old best friend, whose thin body fell limp under the pressure, and felt their classmates staring.

"I've missed you *so* much," Callie blurted uncoolly, but she honestly couldn't help it. After everything that had happened— the E fiasco last spring, Easy coming to visit her in Barcelona over the summer and telling him she loved him, the fact that he hadn't said it back and now might be into her midget-slut room- mate—it was hard to stand in front of Tinsley and maintain composure. Everything about her was so effortless and cool. And no matter how confident Callie was normally, she felt like her roommate's ugly, lame-ass step-cousin when they stood side by side. While she was freckled all over, Tinsley's skin was buttery smooth and naturally tanned; while Callie's strawberry blond hair was flyawayed and unmanageable, Tinsley's jet black hair fell down her back like a heavy sheath. While Callie cared about the gauge of her cashmere sweaters and owning whatever bag Sienna Miller was carrying in that month's British *Vogue*, Tinsley looked incredible in whatever she picked up off the floor. And now, here she was. A million questions ran through Callie's mind: *Where the hell have you been? Why haven't you called me? Is that really a giant shark tooth on your neck?* Finally she whispered a simple: "What happened?"

Tinsley glared at a knot of blond-bobbed sophomores straining their ears to hear from the stone walkway. She took Callie by the arm and walked around to the east side of the chapel.

"Please tell me. What the fuck happened?" Callie couldn't help asking again.

Tinsley leaned her weight against the stone building. "You tell me."

"I don't know." Callie's hands flapped stupidly.

"You didn't set me up?" Tinsley demanded.

Callie shook her head emphatically.

"Did Brett?"

For a split second, Callie considered blaming Brett for everything. That'd serve her right for keeping her teacher lover a secret. But things were getting better between them. Sort of. "It wasn't us."

"Swear?"

"Swear." She stupidly raised her right hand with its chipped South of the Highway pink polished nails. She'd made a mess of them while playing a totally-out-of-character midnight game of Frisbee with some of the dorkier Dumbarton girls last night, hoping to get her mind off Jenny and Easy.

Tinsley looked at her doubtfully, and Callie's lip started to quiver. She wanted everything to be like it was before, when she and Brett and Tinsley were the kind of threesome who finished each other's thoughts and laughed before anyone ever said anything. The kind who trusted each other no matter what. That seemed so long ago now.

"When Marymount asked me about the E, I assumed we were going to share the blame equally," Tinsley finally offered, squinting at her friend. Callie looked like she'd aged five years since the spring. "So I confessed."

Callie gasped, raising her hand to her mouth. "But I denied everything. . . . I thought we all would."

Tinsley noticed her roommate's chewed fingernails and chipped light-pink polish and felt sorry for her even though the situation should have been reversed. "Marymount kicked me out on the spot. *Finito.*"

"Then why did they let you back in?" Callie asked as the last stragglers headed into Chapel for morning meeting, their I-just-rolled-out-of-bed ponytails bobbing as they hurried up the steps.

"They found out I spent break making a documentary with my dad in South Africa and changed my expulsion to a suspension." Tinsley ran her fingers through her glossy dark mane. She wanted to spill all the details about her mind-blowing summer, but not just yet. Callie needed to feel how angry she'd been about being the only one expelled. How unfair it was that they hadn't confessed too and how much it hurt that neither of them had even tried to get in touch with her over the summer. Then, once Callie felt totally incapacitated by guilt, she'd say she was sorry, really sorry, and she'd offer to do *anything* to make it up to her. *Anything.*

A strange, high-pitched whinnying sound broke the silence. *"Nei-ei-ei-ei-gh."*

They both turned their heads to see Heath Ferro whinnying like a horse, BlackBerry in hand. He dragged his foot through the dirt like a disgruntled mule as his thumbs worked the tiny buttons. Callie dug her fingertips into her palms, wincing at the idea that Heath's idiotic party had brought Easy and Jenny closer.

"What's up, good-looking?" Tinsley beckoned teasingly. "Miss me?"

Heath looked up from under his shaggy blondish brown hair

and froze. "Wow. You back?" He grinned devilishly, his gold-flecked green eyes sparkling, and pocketed his BlackBerry.

Callie rolled her eyes. Heath, like every other boy at Waverly and the rest of the Northern Hemisphere, had always had a massive crush on Tinsley, and Callie knew it.

"Yeah, I'm back," Tinsley continued. "For now."

Heath clutched his pocket as his BlackBerry started to vibrate.

"Who's that?" Callie asked.

"Wouldn't you like to know?" Heath replied, pulling out his BlackBerry as a devious smile spread across his face. He shuffled toward the chapel steps, again punching at the tiny keypad. Organ music drifted through the chapel windows and floated out over the soccer field. The quiet muffle of forced singing soon filled the tension-heavy air.

"I just wish . . ." Callie's voice trailed off as she spotted Easy Walsh loping up the walkway, his eyes fixed on a pair of fat owls flying overhead. Callie noticed the splotch of yellow paint on the cuff of his faded Levi's and knew he'd probably been up since dawn, painting in his secret spot in the woods. He'd never told Callie exactly where it was, but she liked to think it was a sunny field of wildflowers in the middle of the forest, where he imagined her lying naked in the grass with dandelions braided into her long, strawberry blond hair, innocent yet totally ravishable. Now she was afraid that Jenny's face was superimposed where hers had been.

"Hey," Tinsley called out, startling Easy. He pretended to do a double take when he saw her—a goofy, exaggerated act Callie had seen him perform time and again, though she never tired of it.

"T-dog," Easy drawled in his irresistible Kentucky accent. He gave them both quick we're-all-good-friends kisses on their cheeks. What the hell? She was not Easy's *friend*. "Where have you been?"

The sunlight darted through the trees overhead, casting shadows on the grass. Callie noticed a new flirtatious lilt in Tinsley's voice as she spoke. Maybe Easy and Tinsley *had* hooked up at last spring, when Ben, the snoopy groundskeeper, spotted the two of them alone out on the halfway line of the soccer field after nightly check-in. Tinsley had nonchalantly denied it when Callie questioned her but in her typical, evasive, could-mean-anything way. And Callie was sure something had happened between the two of them two years ago during freshman year, when Tinsley threw a spring break party at her parents' house in Alaska. But since that predated Callie's relationship with Easy, she couldn't really hold it against either of them. Though it wasn't like she could forget, either.

"Well, it's good to have you back." Easy smiled, his eyelids drooping sexily. Callie felt her insides twist at the sight of his long, dark eyelashes and gorgeous, callused hands. She remembered their roughness caressing her face. "This place has been dying for a dose of you."

"It's good to see you too, Ease." Tinsley drew her tanned foot in a wide, slow-motion arc across the wet grass. Callie narrowed her green-flecked eyes and started up the chapel's stone steps. "Really good," she heard Tinsley say behind her.

"Mr. Walsh." A deep baritone voice sounded from the chapel doorway. In front of Callie stood Mr. Dalton, freshly shaven, his sandy-colored hair still damp and messy from the shower. Callie noticed Easy's body stiffen. Mr. Dalton was the Disciplinary Committee's faculty adviser, and he'd nailed Easy with probation for being in their room that night.

"Mr. Dalton," he replied mechanically, marching up the steps past her and then the history teacher.

"Good morning, ladies." Mr. Dalton nodded at them once as Easy shuffled inside. He smoothed out his maroon-and-navy-striped tie, and Callie noticed a silver link bracelet on his wrist. Ew, wasn't that a little girlie? Then he tilted his head toward Tinsley and offered her his hand. "I'm Eric Dalton. I don't believe we've met."

"Tinsley Carmichael." She stepped onto the bottom stair and gave him her hand in response. "A pleasure."

"Yes." Mr. Dalton nodded enthusiastically. "It is."

Callie still couldn't believe Brett was doing it with a teacher. Ew! She waited for him to disappear back inside Chapel before turning back to Tinsley.

"Who was *that*?" Tinsley asked excitedly, her violet eyes looking even bigger and darker than usual. She pulled her hair over her shoulder and started absentmindedly braiding it.

"Ask Brett," Callie scoffed.

"Where *is* Brett? I need to talk to her too."

Callie shrugged. Let them work their own shit out. This was her turn. She grabbed her friend's bronzed hand, readying herself to apologize before they went inside. It wasn't something Callie was particularly good at, but she wanted to make everything right.

"I just wish we could've planned our stories out before, you know?" she began awkwardly, hugging Tinsley again. "I feel horrible that you got all the blame." She felt a hot tear forming in the corner of her eye and was thankful for the waterproof mascara she'd decided on earlier, anticipating what would happen if she spotted Easy and Jenny together. She buried her face in Tinsley's neck.

"Apology accepted," Tinsley replied evenly, pulling back. "That just leaves one thing."

"What?" Callie blinked away the tear.

"Who's that bitch in my bed?"

"Oh, that's Jenny," Callie replied.

"You're going to help me move her stuff, right?"

Callie smiled. *"Totally."*

OwlNet

RyanReynolds: You at Chapel yet? I'm trying to get close to that Jenny girl. She just snuck in the back door and damn, her skirt is SHORT!

HeathFerro: Guess who I just saw?

RyanReynolds: Jenny? Save me a seat, bro.

HeathFerro: Nope even better. Tinsley fucking SMOKING HOT Carmichael. And I have to tell you, it's a sweeeeeeeeeeeeet sight.

RyanReynolds: Are you fucking with me? I thought that was just a rumor she was coming back.

HeathFerro: Looks like the real thing to me . . .

RyanReynolds: Send me a pic with your camera phone STAT.

HeathFerro: Sorry chump. Don't have one. And I wouldn't share if I did. She and Callie look like they're busy kissing and making up. . . .

RyanReynolds: You definitely need to get a camera.

A WAVERLY OWL NEVER LOSES HER COOL EVEN
WHEN SHE'S REALLY PISSED.

Brett Messerschmidt stood outside the door to room 303, her pointy ivory-colored ankle boots squeezing her toes. She could hear Tinsley's hoarse, sexy voice on the other side of the door, bitching to Callie about how Brett was taking up too much closet space. Brett reread the note her new roommate, Jenny, had written on the door's whiteboard, her whole body trembling with anticipation at the thought of seeing Tinsley again.

Happy Tuesday! Dinner tonight after practice? —J

Jenny was just so . . . *sincere*, like she cared way more about being happy than cool and like she wasn't interested in who your parents were or if they, say, lived in New Jersey or East Hampton. She was basically as different from Tinsley as anyone could possibly be. Brett couldn't stop worrying that it was probably only a matter of time before Tinsley informed everyone on campus about Brett's family. Brett had told everyone her mom and dad had an organic farm in the Hamptons, but the truth was her dad did boob jobs and tummy tucks for a living while her mom reupholstered their Rumson, New Jersey, living room furniture in clashing animal prints.

Even though it hadn't been Callie or Brett's *fault* that Tinsley had been kicked out—neither of them had ratted her out, even though they'd both spent the summer assuming the other had—Brett knew she'd blame them. She rolled her head around on her neck like a boxer getting ready for a fight and pushed open the heavy oak door.

Tinsley stood in the middle of the room, tall and model thin, wearing a turquoise-and-green Ginger and Java strapless silk blouson minidress beneath her maroon Waverly jacket. Brett didn't believe in superstitious insanity like auras, but it sure felt like Tinsley was radiating *something*.

"Well, well," Tinsley said coolly. "Nice to see you, B."

Brett smoothed her Seven jeans skirt, unsure if she should go over and give Tinsley a hug. She had never dealt well with people being mad at her—especially people who might very well spill your deepest, darkest secret just for shits and giggles. "You look fabulous as usual, T."

Callie cleared her throat and slid a thick textbook into her black nylon Prada schoolbag. Her hair was in its usual messy after-practice bun and her hockey clothes were balled up next to the closet. Brett had skipped practice, claiming to have cramps—Coach Smail was super-squeamish when it came to anything period-related—and sat outside Stansfield Hall, hoping to "casually" bump into Eric Dalton leaving his office. No luck.

He might be a teacher and the Disciplinary Committee adviser, but he was also the most incredible . . . *man* . . . Brett had ever met. Last week, after the big Black Saturday game, she'd been absolutely sure that she was ready to lose her virginity to Eric. But then she'd chickened out and run off Eric's yacht and directly into her ex-boyfriend, Jeremiah, who went to nearby St. Lucius Academy. Oops.

"I'll let you two get reacquainted," Callie muttered before heading toward the door. Brettreally wished Callie wouldn't leave. Even if things had been strained between the two of them, Brett was a little scared to be left alone with Tinsley. What if she'd already told Callie she was really just a tacky Jersey girl? What if they'd re-bonded over how idiotically fire-engine red Brett had dyed her hair? What if Tinsley burned a hole in her soul with her freaky violet eyes?

"Thanks for helping me with my stuff, Cal." Tinsley puckered her bee-stung lips and made an exaggerated air smooch before she gently closed the door behind her. Brett wondered if Callie would stick around to eavesdrop on their conversation like Brett had. Probably.

Tinsley's Louis Vuitton luggage was piled onto her old bed, and a tiny metal-framed cot, sagging slightly in the middle, was pushed into the corner where the girls normally stashed their trash can. Jenny's comforter and sheets were tangled in a ball on top of it. One of her pillows was on the floor.

Tinsley looked at Brett, standing ramrod straight across the room. Her pointy little nose was as red as her insanely dyed hair, which Tinsley recognized as a sign she was nervous. What was her fucking deal? She couldn't even muster up a little excitement about seeing her old best friend back where she belonged, *especially* after she had saved her ass? Where was the gratitude? The respect? The *fawning*? She had just gotten back from another hemisphere, for Christ's sake, not the dining hall. "You're looking pale," Tinsley finally initiated.

Brett walked over to her desk and draped her size-two Waverly blazer over her chair. "I'm not feeling well," she replied primly.

Tinsley tugged at the zipper on her signature leather garment bag and pulled out an armful of chiffon and silk. She narrowed her carefully made-up eyes at Brett as she walked to the closet and slid Brett's things out of the way. It made Tinsley think of all the times the three of them had faked day passes from their parents and taken the train into the city to shop at Barneys and the boutiques in Soho. Tinsley even spotted the silver Missoni slip dress she'd dared her to shoplift from Saks. *Fuck you,* Tinsley wanted to yell. *Just apologize and kiss my ass a little so we can all be friends again!* But Brett was just standing there stubbornly, running her finger along the collection of small gold hoops in her left ear. What did *she* have to be pissed about? "Still going out with Jeremiah?" Tinsley finally asked.

"That's over." Brett cleared her throat and willed herself not to think about Eric Dalton. Tinsley had some sort of extrasensory perception when it came to secrets, and as soon as she sensed anything surreptitious, she'd latch on until she'd uncovered every juicy detail.

"Oh, yeah? So, who's the next victim?" Tinsley asked pointedly, thinking of Mr. Dalton and his sexy gray eyes and monogrammed platinum cuff links and the way Callie suggested she ask Brett about him. She knew her friends, and she knew what that meant. He had to be *quite* a score for a closeted Jersey girl like Brett.

"That remains to be seen." Brett turned to start gathering her books. "Look, I'm on my way to Benny's to study. I was just stopping by to get some things," she lied.

Tinsley bristled. Since when did Brett care more about hitting the books with horse-faced Benny Cunningham than welcoming back her long-lost friend?

"I was going to check out what Brandon and Heath were doing anyway," Tinsley responded casually. Now, there would be some faces happy to see her. She grabbed her oversized tangerine-colored Prada tote and headed for the door. "Maybe I'll see you around."

She shut it loudly, scattering the girls who had been eavesdropping, and waited in the hall until she heard Brett murmur, "*Bitch.*"

Bitch? she mused, clicking down the hall. *Well, we'll see what Mr. Too-hot-to-be-a-teacher Dalton thinks of bitches.*

OwlNet

TinsleyCarmichael: Wts the deal with the insanely hot new guy?

BennyCunningham: The super-tall one from Seattle? Looks delicious but he's a freshman! Unfair right?

TinsleyCarmichael: The dude is definitely not a freshman. Dalton or something?

BennyCunningham: U mean MISTER Dalton? He's a history teacher and does DC.

TinsleyCarmichael: I think he's my adviser.

BennyCunningham: Lucky bitch. I heard he and Brett were playing footsie at the last DC meeting.

TinsleyCarmichael: Très interesting . . .

To: JennyHumphrey@Waverly.edu
From: RufusHumphrey@poetsonline.com
Date: Tuesday, September 9, 3:14 p.m.
Subject: New phone

Hello, my jalapeño pumpkin fritter,

I got your letter from last week. I'm still amazed by the email. Incredible!

Dan is settling into Evergreen. He hasn't ended up in the infirmary with a case of alcohol poisoning or spinal meningitis or homesickness yet, so I think we're off to a good start.

So you asked for a Tripod or a Treon or something? I didn't know what this was, so I asked Vanessa—she's living in your room . . . did I remember to tell you that?—and she brought me to the cell phone store. I waxed philosophic and showed off my I Break for Salamanders pin and rainbow suspenders, so the salesgirl cut me a deal. And you think I have no fashion sense. Keep an eye out for a duct-taped shoe box coming via snail mail!

Love you to the moon,

Dad

A WAVERLY OWL IS A VERY,

VERY TRUSTWORTHY OWL.

Jenny jogged back to Dumbarton after field hockey practice, enjoying the wholesome ache in her muscles and the view of the sprawling green campus, the ancient brick buildings, the preppy, pink-cheeked students. All the compulsory exercise she was getting made her feel like one of the lithe, blond, ponytailed girls doing playful cartwheels on the Waverly Academy Web site, though her hair was brown and curly and she was barely five feet tall. After fifteen years in New York City, she'd been shocked to discover she possessed any degree of athletic talent beyond hailing a taxi, but here she was, playing *varsity* field hockey at *boarding school*.

She wanted to call up her brother in Washington to brag as soon as she got her new cell phone, but she knew Dan wouldn't be at all impressed. He'd probably accuse her of being a cliché or something equally mean. Jenny inhaled the late-afternoon air, with its hints of freshly mown grass and woodstove burning off in the distance. She swore she could smell the leaves changing color. She decided to email Dan later about the leaves and not mention the exercise. He was a poet. Poets liked leaves.

"Hey, sexy," a lazy, stoned-sounding voice called out. Jenny whirled around and saw Heath Ferro lying on his back on one of the long stone benches that were artfully scattered across campus, each with a plaque naming the Waverly alum who had donated it. "Why don'tcha come over here and sit down?" He patted his lap. "Where are you running to, anyway?"

"Away from you!" Jenny called playfully without stopping. She'd kissed him inside the chapel on her very first night at Waverly, and then he'd told everyone they'd done a lot more than that. Apparently Heath really got around, so much so the girls had taken to calling him Pony because, as it had been somewhat ickily explained to her, he got more ass than a pony at the country fair.

She might still be upset about it, but then she'd managed to turn it all back around during the biggest field hockey game of the fall, called Black Saturday, when Waverly played its rival St. Lucius. Callie had given her some made-up lyrics to a cheer that were kind of dirty and a little embarrassing, but Jenny had gotten so into them that she'd spontaneously added a line of her own. She sang it to herself now as she ran along the ancient stone path leading up to Dumbarton: *"There is a boy who they call Pony! He's always acting gross and horny! He thinks he's got a lot down there, but he sure wears tiny underwear!"* She'd gotten back at Heath with that, and even if Heath *was* a sleazebag, it still felt good to be able to catch the eye of one of the best-looking guys at Waverly. God, she loved this place!

Jenny rushed into room 303 with her adrenaline still high and found her roommate Brett sitting on the window ledge, staring at an owl perched in the maple tree across the lawn. "Hey, Brett," she greeted her, still out of breath. That's when she saw her bed was covered with Louis Vuitton luggage. Jenny almost yelped. "Whose stuff is that on my bed?"

"I think Tinsley's been rearranging things," Brett offered quietly. "I thought you knew. . . ."

"I knew she was here, but I didn't know she was going to just move my stuff like that!" Their encounter that morning had been brief and startlingly unpleasant. Now the sight of her neatly made bed stripped and piled high with Tinsley's expensive luggage and her own blankets crumpled up and tossed onto a flimsy, sagging cot made her furious. She picked her pillow up off the floor and slapped the dust off it while she tried to calm herself down. "That's just not fair."

Brett shrugged and held her Urban Decay Acid Rain painted eyelids closed for a moment. "I really can't picture Tinsley sleeping on a cot, though. . . ."

Uch! She'd never known anyone with violet eyes, except for Elizabeth Taylor, who was the most beautiful movie star she could imagine before she got old and kind of fat, but Jenny didn't care how beautiful Tinsley was—this was just plain *mean*. But if it made Tinsley happy to have her old bed back, then she might as well have it. Jenny just wished she'd asked first and that she herself didn't have to sleep on a cot that smelled like the musty basement it must have just come from.

"We missed you at practice today," Jenny said, perching on

her saggy, stupid cot to take off her soggy field hockey socks. Then she felt like a phony because she hadn't even noticed that Brett wasn't at practice until she walked into their dorm room and saw her sitting there, still dressed in her tight green cashmere sweater and ivory ankle boots. It was Tuesday, and Jenny had had her portraiture class before practice, meaning she had spent the afternoon sitting next to Easy, drawing and sharing glances and passing notes, and for the rest of the afternoon she had been unable to think of anything but him. Just being near him made Jenny feel kind of blissful and totally forgetful about things . . . like how he was still going out with Callie.

Jenny took the ball of bedding off the cot and started pulling her fitted sheet around the small, flimsy cot mattress. It fit like saggy granny underwear.

The sound of a band of freshmen singing "Drop It Like It's Hot" at the top of their lungs drifted through the open window. Brett was still staring absentmindedly at the Hudson. Jenny walked over and sat down on Brett's unmade bed. Neither Brett nor Callie made their beds, but Jenny wasn't comfortable enough to leave her sheets and blanket in a tangle like they did. That would be like letting them see her bra, and it was definitely too soon for that. She was still changing in the bathroom.

"You okay?" Jenny asked, not wanting to disturb her, but also not wanting to be the kind of roommate who didn't ask if everything was okay, when something was so clearly not okay. "Coach said you were sick."

Brett turned her head toward Jenny. "Something like that."

There was a reason she felt queasy: Eric. Sure, he was

technically a teacher, but he wasn't *her* teacher. When he took her home to Lindisfarne, his family estate in Newport, Rhode Island, last week and they sat on the porch of the guesthouse, it didn't take more than a sip of vintage bordeaux that was older than she was before she blurted out the truth about her family. And Eric Dalton—a Waverly legacy, heir to a veritable American dynasty, with his gorgeous, classy Newport house and gorgeous, classy blue-blood New England family—made her feel intriguing and sexy in spite of her classless upbringing.

Brett tucked her fiery hair behind her ears. Jenny was so sweet, sitting there at the edge of her bed, as if she were afraid of disturbing it. It was no wonder everyone was talking about how Easy Walsh was in love with her. Brett didn't know if it was true, but she could definitely see how it could happen.

Brett flopped down on her bed next to Jenny, their knees bumping. "You have to swear you won't tell anyone, okay?" She had only known Jenny for a week now, but Brett had been feeling friendless this year, with Tinsley away and Callie acting like a complete ice queen. And now Tinsley and Callie seemed like they were back to being BFF and were probably plotting to ruin her life. Besides, Jenny already knew about Eric since she'd seen Brett sneaking back into the room in the middle of the night last week.

"I promise." Jenny drew a cross over her heart.

"Good, because you know how it is when you like someone so much, you just can't stop thinking about them, and all you want to do is talk about them?" Brett bit the corner of her lip. There was probably at least a *little* truth to the rumors about Jenny and Easy. Jenny *had* to understand.

"Yeah," Jenny said quietly. "I do." Jenny remembered gazing at the stars with Easy at Heath's party when he told her he wanted to be in love like in the De Beers diamond ads. He'd been embarrassed about saying it, but Jenny had known just what he meant. He'd said he didn't have that now—meaning he didn't have it with Callie—but that he wanted it. She wondered if maybe he wanted it with *her*.

"Well, you know about this . . . *thing* . . . going on with . . ." Brett peered closely at Jenny. "You know." Jenny nodded, so Brett kept going. "But the thing is, he's not returning my texts or calls."

"How long has it been since you guys talked?"

Brett pretended to have to think about it, but she knew exactly how long it had been. "Two days. I've called him twice." Eleven times, actually, but she didn't want Jenny to think she was obsessive.

Outside, the same girls who had been singing "Drop It Like It's Hot" started loudly elaborating on which Waverly boys were the cutest. "Easy Walsh is so hot!" wafted up to the room, and Jenny's face immediately flushed.

Brett smiled. It looked like Jenny definitely had a secret of her own.

OwlNet

CelineColista: B, I couldn't finish my paper on Herodotus. U think Dalton will give me an extension?

BrettMesserschmidt: How would I know? I'm not in your class.

CelineColista: Well u guys are friends, right? Maybe you could put in a good word for me?

BrettMesserschmidt: I work with him on DC . . . so do you.

CelineColista: But don't you have, like, private meetings?

BrettMesserschmidt: DC business only.

CelineColista: That's too bad. I mean, for my extension.

5

A WAVERLY OWL DOES NOT ENGAGE IN HALLUCINO-
GENIC ACTIVITIES, ORGANIC OR OTHERWISE.

"How good did Tinsley look? Like, Jessica Alba in *Sin City* hot?" Ryan Reynolds asked pleadingly. "What was she *wearing*? Why have I not seen her yet?"

Brandon Buchanan set his sleek black squash bag down on the worn yet polished hardwood floor of the Richards common room. Even draped with teenage boys, the room felt like an old English hunting lodge, with its dark mahogany moldings, forest green walls, and bookshelves filled with leather-bound volumes of classics no one had ever heard of. It kind of made Brandon wish he had one of his father's pipes.

He rolled his eyes at Julian McCafferty, the tall, long-haired freshman from Seattle who had just come from squash practice with him. Brandon had beaten him, of course, but it was a little too close for him to feel comfortable. Normally, that would have been enough to make Brandon avoid him, but Julian was surprisingly cool. Girls were going to like him too, Brandon thought a little jealously, once he cut his caveman hair.

"Who's Tinsley?" Julian asked in a mock whisper. As always, the room was crowded with zoned-out boys, exhausted from sports practice and re-acclimating to school life after their relaxing summers at their country and beach houses. ESPN flashed from the cabinet television in the corner, the sound muted, Brandon assumed, so that they could all gossip about Tinsley. They were worse than girls.

Everyone chuckled at Julian's ignorance. "Dude, clearly you're a freshman," said Alan St. Girard, the crunchy junior whose parents both taught philosophy at expensive East Coast liberal arts colleges and reportedly owned a marijuana plantation in New Hampshire. He had bushy brown hair and perpetual beard scruff, which the girls found endearing but Brandon thought disgusting. Fucking shave, dude. "She's only the foxiest girl on the planet."

"Isn't there something in the handbook about her?" asked Teague Williams, his post-soccer practice body dripping sweat on one of the expensive leather armchairs. "Like, 'Male Waverly Owls, beware this girl. She will tease you and torture you and haunt your dreams with her luscious presence all four years at Waverly and for the rest of your life on earth.'"

"I can't wait to meet her." Julian dropped his maroon Nike squash bag onto the floor and pulled his bleached-out dirty blond hair into a ponytail, using the rubber band he kept on his wrist to secure it. Brandon shuddered with distaste. "What's she look like?"

The guys gave a collective sigh, and Brandon sank into one of the ancient armchairs. Tinsley was hot, but these guys were ridiculous. She was nowhere near as beautiful as Callie, who Brandon had dated all of freshman year before Easy fucking Walsh stole her from him. They'd been at a party in the library, and when he'd gone to go get Callie a drink, like the gentleman that he was, Easy had swooped in and dragged her up to the rare books room and put some kind of southern cowboy spell on her. And now there were all kinds of rumors that he was leaving Callie for Jenny Humphrey, the cute new girl who Brandon had thought could actually get him over Callie. Fucking Walsh. He shot an angry look at Easy's sprawled-out, horsey-smelling body on the scratchy plaid couch.

"Don't get your hopes up, kid," said Ryan as he made room on the couch for Julian to sit. "Tinsley doesn't even talk to freshmen."

"Now that she's back, I have a feeling this year just got a whole lot more interesting," drawled Easy without looking up from the sketchbook on his lap. Brandon fought the urge to roll his eyes. Was there a girl on campus that Easy was *not* into? First Callie, then Jenny, now Tinsley? There were rumors he and Tinsley had hooked up at her parents' house in Alaska spring break freshman year, but Easy had never confirmed the story, not that Brandon even cared.

"Hell, yeah!" Everyone turned to see Heath Ferro standing in the doorway with a wicked grin on his handsome face. "I was just talking to my cousin who graduated from here, like, five years ago, and he told me something freaking *awesome*. He said that if you walk to the other side of the crater, it gets all swampy

and shit, and guess what's growing there?" Heath looked at everyone expectantly, as though anything he was saying made sense.

"'Shrooms, dudes!" he yelled. "I thought we'd head over to the
woods and enjoy some natural highs, Alice in Wonderland style. It
has been a long week," he added, even though it was only Tuesday.
"So who's in?" Heath snapped his fingers impatiently.

Ryan and Alan immediately bumped fists with him.
"We're in."

Brandon groaned and ran his hands through his freshly show-
ered and gelled hair. "It's fucking Tuesday. I've got five chapters
of *Tess of the D'Urbervilles* to read for tomorrow."

"Oh, poor Brandon!" Heath snickered in the falsetto he
reserved for making fun of his roommate's girly attributes. "Not
five chapters!"

"Fuck off, Ferro. Not everyone's daddies can buy them A's."

"If freshmen aren't banned, I'd love to partake." Julian's deep
baritone boomed as he stood up. It was so unfair for a freshman
to be so fucking tall and manly. When Brandon was a freshman,
he was barely five-foot two and his voice sounded like a girl's.

Easy dropped his sketchbook to the floor and uncrossed his
legs. "Why not?"

Brandon sighed under his breath. Although he wanted to
spend as little time as possible around the loathsome Walsh, he
wasn't about to let Easy and some novice freshman make him
look like a pussy. "Fine. Let's get out of here," he relented.
Thomas Hardy was meant to be skimmed anyway.

Easy and Alan tossed a Frisbee back and forth, reminding
Brandon of a couple of sloppy golden retrievers, as the group

crossed campus to the patch of woods separating the brick buildings from the river. Preppy boys and girls with backpacks and
cable-knit sweaters hustled off to the library for a few hours of
cramming before curfew, and Brandon wished he could just sit
with Callie again on the library steps like they used to, talking
and flirting and making out when no one was looking. Instead,
he was going hunting for 'shrooms with a bunch of jackass guys,
one of whom had actually stolen the girl he loved from him and
was possibly now on the verge of breaking her heart.

Brandon's calfskin Gucci loafers padded down the path
through the woods until Heath and Easy stepped off the stone
path and into the brush. Brandon tried not to ruin his shoes as
they picked their way through the tall weeds and low branches.
The woods opened briefly onto a small clearing filled with large
rocks that students had been using as a clandestine party spot for
decades—the crater. The sky above was darkening, but it wasn't
yet cold.

"He said to look for the biggest rock along the edge and then
walk into the woods until it gets soppy." Heath identified the
biggest rock and motioned to them like he was flagging in a
plane on the runway.

Brandon frowned at his shoes. The parade of boys crunched
the sticks and leaves underfoot, and then suddenly the earth got
spongy and damp. "Fuck," Brandon muttered under his breath.

"Behold!" Heath crouched at the base of a tree. "Mushrooms!"

Everyone started to pick them, gathering the dirty caps in
their hands. Brandon would have expected them to look a little

more exotic. These looked so innocent and, well, culinary, as if they belonged in some kind of Szechuan stir-fry his family's cook, Greta, might throw together.

"Hate to break it to you, Ferro." Ryan nibbled on one of the caps and then sniffed it as though he was a mushroom connoisseur, which, given the rumors about his parents, was possible. "But these aren't the real thing."

"Shit, man," Heath muttered. "Well, should we chill at the crater or head back?"

Disappointed votes to chill were murmured, and a few minutes later Brandon felt the cold wetness of the grass soaking through his Dolce & Gabbana jeans as the rest of the guys revisited the topic of Tinsley's hotness. Brandon closed his eyes and let the sound of the crickets drown out the boys' voices. He really wasn't interested in thinking about Tinsley. He loved *Callie*. She'd dumped him for Easy over a year ago, so they'd been broken up for longer than they'd been together, but still Brandon couldn't get her off his mind. And she wasn't helping much—last week he'd bumped into her after one of the girls-only welcome-back parties and she'd drunkenly asked him to sleep with her. He'd just wanted to hold her and talk to her until the alcohol wore off. He would have sat up with her all night, but he wasn't about to take advantage of her when she was clearly an emotional wreck about whatever was going on with that slimeball Easy. Sleazy Easy.

"The stars are coming out. Chicks love stars," Heath remarked. "You know who I'd take here?"

"Tinsley," a few of the guys said in unison.

"Good luck with that, Ferro," Easy drawled. He was lying on the grass, staring at the sky. Callie had named a star for him once through some cheesy Web site, but looking at the sky right now, he couldn't imagine looking for his star with Callie. The only girl he wanted to look at stars with was Jenny. If only she were here right now.

"We should head back." Brandon interrupted Easy's thoughts, and the boys stumbled awkwardly to their feet, still talking about Tinsley and what it would be like to be with her. Easy *had* been with her, before Callie, when a bunch of them went up to Alaska for spring break. They'd stayed up all night, naked in the hot tub, mostly just talking and looking at the stars. Tinsley was gorgeous, but Easy was pretty sure that the thing that made guys obsess over her was the same thing that made him happy to stay away. She was kind of . . . *wicked*.

Then, as they stepped back onto the manicured green of the main campus, Easy saw Tinsley marching toward them across the grass. He watched her approach, wearing a strapless turquoise minidress and black cloth Mary Janes like the kind you buy in tacky Chinese gift shops. Leave it to Tinsley to pair a dress like that with five-dollar shoes.

"Don't you all look suspicious, coming out of the woods like this," she observed provocatively. "What were you *doing* in there?" she continued when the boys were close enough to smell her sweet and musky perfume.

"Secret society meeting," Easy replied mysteriously. His almost-black curls hung sloppily in his face, embedded with crushed leaves. "You wouldn't understand."

Tinsley smacked his stomach with the back of her hand. "Oh, yeah? What do you do? Smoke pot and talk about girls?" Her violet eyes gleamed. Tinsley could always sniff out a secret. "Can I come next time?"

"Sorry, lady." Easy grinned, speaking for all of them. "Gentlemen only."

"Well, that's *stupid*," Tinsley pronounced, her lips forming a pink pout. "I guess I'll have to start my own secret society, then." She stuck out her tongue before turning away, a master at leaving her audience gasping for more.

6

A WAVERLY OWL MUST OBEY CURFEW, BUT THAT
DOESN'T MEAN YOU CAN'T STAY UP ALL NIGHT.

Brett's silver Nokia vibrated noisily against the wooden dresser as both she and Jenny raised their eyes from their Norton anthologies and stared at each other. Brett's bright-green, cat-like eyes gleamed triumphantly as she dashed over to the phone and read the caller ID. "Finally!" she yelped before taking a deep breath and attempting to remove all excitement from her voice. "Yes," she answered coolly as Jenny giggled and pulled her Nick and Nora flannel cherry-print pajama-clad knees to her chest.

"Can you meet me at my place in Rhinecliff? I have to see you." Eric's deep voice immediately erased any worry she'd been feeling, as if he had just tucked aside her hair and spoken softly, breathily into her ear. She felt her face heat up, and Jenny gestured toward the door and mouthed, "Should I go?"

Brett shook her head before turning toward the window and

looking out at the darkening evening. It was nine-fifteen. Less than an hour to curfew.

"How will I get there?" Brett responded finally, looking down at her pale pink silky La Perla camisole and favorite pair of super-soft black C&C California yoga pants that she wore on days she was feeling fat or depressed.

"I'll send a car for you. Be at the front gate in twenty minutes, okay?"

Brett hung up quickly and immediately started tugging off her pants. "I knew he'd call," she squealed, pulling a pair of dark James jeans out of the depths of her closet. She kept on her camisole since she was wearing the matching underwear and she automatically felt much sexier when wearing a complete set. Brett stared at herself in the mirror. Her face was clean of makeup since she had already performed her nightly pore-cleansing ritual. She spread a layer of DuWop lip venom across her naked lips, enjoying the way it tingled. Then she stepped into a pair of pink Marc Jacobs ballet flats and pulled on a romantic-looking brown velveteen blazer from Anthropologie. "Do I look all right?"

Jenny didn't know what to say. "Uh, you're going out? *Now?*"

"No one will know. Don't mention where I am to Callie and Tinsley, okay?"

Brett looked beautiful—clean and sweet and delicate—but Jenny still wasn't so sure how she felt about her with Mr. Dalton. She knew Brett was way worldlier than she was, but there was something kind of skeezy about it all. Yet standing in front of the mirror, adjusting her red hair behind her ears, Brett seemed to positively glow. Who was Jenny to be the unwelcome voice of reason when Brett was clearly happier than she'd been all week?

"Sure, I'll make something up," Jenny said, standing up to brush a fleck of lint off Brett's shoulder. "You look really pretty."

Brett twirled out of the room in a cloud of romantic exhilaration, but a knot of nerves settled in her stomach as she slipped into the black Town Car that was waiting for her outside Waverly's front gate. The driver didn't say anything to her, and Brett suddenly felt like the mistress of some wealthy banker dude, being summoned while his bitchy wife was away at the spa.

After passing through the sleepy main street of the tiny town of Rhinecliff, the car turned toward the river and drove along a thickly wooded road. Lights from large, tasteful homes glinted through the trees. Then, right when it looked like they were about to drive into the slow-moving Hudson, the car turned suddenly down a long driveway. Branches swept lightly against the windows and sides of the car. Completely private, Brett noted.

The car pulled up in front of a modern angular redwood-and-glass house nestled into the riverbank. Eric opened the front door, wearing Diesel jeans and a navy blue vintage Red Sox T-shirt. Seeing him dressed so casually felt so intimate. He looked exactly like the kind of beautiful yet faintly scruffy college student she'd always dreamed about bumping into on one of her many Ivy League college tours. The Red Sox logo made her think guiltily of Jeremiah before she quickly pushed him out of her mind.

"I'm sorry for not calling. I've been so busy." Eric leaned in to give Brett a kiss on the cheek, lingering longer than necessary. "I've missed you, and you smell lovely."

Brett hated to swoon, but how many boys did she know who could say "lovely" in all seriousness? Certainly not Jeremiah. She immediately forgave Eric for all the unreturned calls. He was an adult, after all. He got busy.

Eric led her through the narrow entryway that opened into a dimly lit living room with cathedral ceilings. A wall of windows looked out on what must have been a breathtaking view of the river, though only blackness was visible now. The room was sparsely and elegantly furnished with low, rectangular pieces of furniture that had clearly been custom-designed for this house. Candles flickered on the coffee table and the sound of saxophone music filled the air.

"Is this a Frank Lloyd Wright house?" she asked, since Frank Lloyd Wright was the only modern architect she knew.

"Nah," Eric said, pouring red wine into the two crystal glasses already sitting on the coffee table. "My grandfather was a big fan of Wright's work but not his lifestyle." He gestured toward the couch, and Brett sat down, wondering what "his lifestyle" meant but too shy to ask. The couch was surprisingly stiff and uncomfortable. She tried leaning against one of the velvety pillows and felt a little better, although she was worried her posture looked too suggestive. Eric handed her a glass and sat next to her, close enough that their knees brushed against each other. "My grandfather was kind of a hard-ass."

"It sounds like your grandfather was a man of . . . *principle*," Brett said, trying to sound sophisticated but suspecting that she sounded like a freak. She sipped her wine and felt a little out of place.

"*He* thought he was," Eric said with a chuckle, setting his glass down on the table. He raised one of his perfectly shaped blond eyebrows and met her gaze. "But he had a weakness for pretty girls."

"Oh?" She could feel herself blushing. She gripped her knees with her hands. "Does that run in the family?"

Eric leaned toward her and tenderly pushed back a strand of Brett's red hair, making sure it didn't snag on any of the small gold hoops she always wore along the upper curve of her left ear. "Just pretty redheads," he murmured hoarsely into her ear.

His fingers slipped down to her shoulder. Brett was having serious trouble concentrating.

"Um . . . Eric? What, exactly, are we doing here?" she faltered, trying to sound as un-childish and casual as possible. "I mean, seriously. You could get in a lot of trouble. We both—"

Eric sighed and took his hand from Brett's shoulder, letting it fall to the back of the couch instead. His sandy blond hair looked darker in the candlelight, and his face turned serious. "I've been thinking about it a lot, and while there are plenty of logical reasons why this shouldn't be happening, I don't want it to stop."

Brett couldn't help herself. She pressed her small knee against his larger one. The sight of their two denim knees together just seemed so normal and right to her. He was just a guy, after all, handsome and smart and totally irresistible. She slowly moved her hand over to his leg and rested it there, admiring the feel of his muscled thigh beneath her shimmering light lavender nails. Suppressing a giggle, she remembered the name of the Hard Candy polish she had picked out of Callie's makeup bag: Jailbait.

"I just . . ." Eric shrugged and brushed an invisible piece of hair off his face. "I just think you're the most amazing girl I've ever met."

She felt drunk even though she'd hardly touched her wine. She moved her face toward his, slowly, keeping her eyes focused on his lips. Finally she met his lips with hers and felt an electric sensation course through her.

After a long, lingering kiss, he pressed his lips to her throat. She couldn't help remembering the last time they were together, on his boat, when they had started taking off each other's clothes. There she was, completely naked in Eric's bed, when she suddenly realized she wasn't ready to do it yet. But this time, she was sure. Who better to share her first time with than someone so incredible . . . who thought she was *amazing*?

But as Eric breathed into her neck and his hands inched toward her breasts, she couldn't help feeling, once again, that he was just *too* good at this. He knew exactly how to touch her, which was, in a way, hypnotically exciting. But whenever she started to think too much about it, which she couldn't help doing, she could picture him doing the exact same thing with some generic girl in her place, who he called amazing and maybe even made the same joke to about the family weakness for red-heads, or blondes, or freckles, or whatever the girl happened to have. How many girls—or *women*—had he been with on this very couch, in this candlelit living room? The thought made her immediately self-conscious, and her body froze up.

Eric pulled away from her and looked at her face questioningly. "I—I think I might not be ready just yet," she stammered, feeling like the biggest baby in the world. She stared at her lap and concentrated on holding back the tears that threatened to come spilling out.

"That's fine, Brett." Eric placed his hands on her cheeks. "Look at me—don't worry about it. There's no hurry—we'll take it slow."

Brett looked up. "I'm sorry I'm such a . . . ," she started to say.

"A what? A beautiful, sexy girl?" He laughed, and Brett smiled sheepishly. "Trust me, I'm not going anywhere. We can take our time." He held out his arms, and Brett collapsed against him in relief, enjoying how his body felt wrapped, fully clothed, around hers. She'd be ready soon; she could tell. Just not yet.

Two hours later, Brett lay partially clothed with Eric dozing next to her, beneath smooth Egyptian cotton sheets that had to be like a thousand thread count. And as nice and sexy and sweet as it was, Brett couldn't help thinking about how her own bed would feel at that moment. She could almost hear the soft whimpering noises Callie made in her sleep. Eric's manly snores kind of reminded her of her father. She wished she had just slept with him and gotten her first time over with—she wouldn't feel like such a kid, and it would make the next time even easier. Needing to pee, she slipped out from under his arm, careful not to wake him.

She reached for the pair of Ralph Lauren silk pajama bottoms on his bureau to pull on over her underwear. As she tightened the drawstring around her waist, a streak of moonlight illuminated the top of the dresser. Next to Eric's sleek black Italian leather wallet lay a plastic baggie of marijuana. Brett picked it up and sniffed inside to be sure. Eric, a pothead? Brett had never smoked pot, but it occurred to her that it might be just what she needed to relax enough to do it with Eric. Maybe next time.

"Where're you going?" Brett turned around to see Eric sitting up in bed, his sexy gray eyes sleepy and his hair rumpled. "You're not leaving?"

"Bathroom," Brett answered, suddenly wondering how she was supposed to get home.

"Spend the night." Eric yawned adorably. "I just want you to sleep next to me."

Brett melted. Without a thought of curfews or her roommates or what she'd wear in the morning, she agreed. "I'd like that too."

OwlNet   Instant Message Inbox

SageFrancis: U awake yet? I just knocked on Pardee's door to tell her our toilet's clogged again and I heard Mr. Pardee totally freaking inside.

BennyCunningham: U get anything good?

SageFrancis: Not really. Maybe she's got a boyfriend? Mr. Dalton?

BennyCunningham: Doubt it. Someone saw Brett getting dropped off at dawn in a schmancy Town Car this morning.

SageFrancis: U don't say . . .

OwlNet Email Inbox

To: EasyWalsh@waverly.edu
From: CallieVernon@waverly.edu
Date: Wednesday, September 11, 9:01 a.m.
Subject: Stables

Hey, baby,

Meet me at the stables at 5 p.m.?

Xxx,

C

A WAVERLY OWL DOES NOT LUST AFTER A ROOM-MATE'S BOYFRIEND—UNTIL AFTER THEY BREAK UP.

Jenny plopped her giant purple suede tote bag she'd gotten at an open-air market in Prague that summer on the floor beneath the art desk she'd tentatively claimed as her own. She'd fallen in love with the bag, and her mother had quickly handed over the two thousand koruny the vendor wanted for it without even trying to bargain, as if her willingness to buy Jenny the bag made her a less-neglectful mother after basically abandoning her and Dan when they were kids. Jenny loved the bag despite its being a bribe and despite its being slightly grungy and not exactly hip. After her first week at Waverly, Jenny was finding herself less concerned with everyone else's idea of what coolness was. There was something very empowering about the way she had found herself turning the Black Saturday cheer to her advantage instead of collapsing in shame, and she suddenly felt like she could do the same with everything if she set her mind to it. Who cared if her bag was slightly lumpy and Eastern Bloc looking?

Yesterday Mrs. Silver had invited Jenny, Easy, and Alison Quentin into the Advanced Portraiture elective that met on Wednesdays. The class was mostly seniors, so Jenny felt especially proud. And the fact that she was going to have another class with Easy didn't hurt either.

Jenny headed to the student supply closet and pulled her enormous newsprint sketch pad out from the shelf labeled HUMPHREY in her elegant calligraphy. She couldn't help smiling at the sight of Easy's name on his shelf in sloppy charcoal, the dark, dusty letters already smearing on the white label.

"Glad you could join us, Mr. Walsh," Mrs. Silver greeted Easy as he strolled into the classroom just as she was closing the door.

"The pleasure is all mine." Easy slid onto the stool next to Jenny, glancing at her out of the corner of his brilliant blue eyes. It was a mixed blessing, a tease, like someone waving a slice of Original Ray's cheese-and-pepperoni pizza under her nose and she was on a diet. What was wrong with her? She didn't know if he and Callie were still together, but either way, Callie was her *roommate*. "Hey," he whispered, barely audibly.

"Hey," Jenny whispered back. What was she doing? She had to force herself to stop flirting with him. Concentrate on her art-work, something!

"I think you have all mastered the basic proportions of the face, working with a mirror and your own reflections." Mrs. Silver, a graying Mrs.-Claus-goes-hippie type, smiled kindly at the class. "Now, I'd like you to work on capturing a likeness of someone else's face. These two rows, pair up with the person next to you—" She pointed at Easy and Jenny's rows. "And these two . . ."

Jenny stopped listening. Easy was already turning his desk to face hers. It was almost as if everyone in the world had united to try and torture her.

"Who wants to go first?" he asked, his pencil already doodling on his paper.

"I'll do you first," Jenny said, not ready for him to be drawing her face yet. She'd blush like an idiot the whole time. Besides, she didn't want him to start comparing her looks to Callie's—she'd never measure up. Callie was the kind of girl who got all primped just to head out to field hockey practice and spend a few hours sweating. Callie was *beautiful*. Jenny looked down at her own less-than-perfect body with her disproportionately large chest and wondered again why he would ever even consider going from being part of such a glamorous couple to being with a girl more than a foot shorter than him. They'd look like freaks!

"All right, but I've never been a model before, so I might not be too good at it." He looked vaguely embarrassed by the whole situation, tapping his fingers nervously on his drawing table.

"It's okay; you don't have to pose or anything." Jenny giggled. "You can talk or draw if you want as long as you don't move too much. And keep your eyes up."

Easy met her eyes, and a slow grin spread across his face. "Okay, boss."

She looked down at her paper and started her preliminary

sketch of the outline of his head with a stub of vine charcoal, but her eyes were immediately drawn back to his face. With only a few glances down at the paper as she sketched, Jenny studied his features more closely than she had before, appreciating the small bump in his nose, the way his big blue eyes turned up at the corners, his slightly uneven sticky-outy ears. Her paper filled up quickly.

"Good," Mrs. Silver said from behind Jenny's desk. "Excellent—class, see how Jenny is keeping her eyes on Easy's face, not buried in her paper? I want you to concentrate on what you are *seeing*, and the drawing will fall into place."

Perfect, Jenny thought. More mixed messages—she couldn't keep her eyes off Easy and she was getting praise for it.

"You were almost late today," Jenny remarked after Mrs. Silver passed on to the next pair, wanting to end the silence between them. She had an itch on her nose but didn't want to scratch it because her fingers were black with charcoal.

"I was out with Credo. The weather's been so sweet, I want to ride as much as possible." Easy's face always lit up when he talked about his horse. Jenny had grown up with lots of girls whose families had houses and stables out in Westchester and Connecticut and who talked about their prize jumpers as if they were in love with them or something. Maybe her anarchist dad had rubbed off on her, but she'd always found them, with their jodhpurs and sleek riding boots, way too pretentious. Or maybe she was just jealous.

"I've never been horseback riding," she admitted, flipping to another page of newsprint and starting a new sketch. She traded her vine charcoal for a soft graphite pencil and set to work on the shape of his eyes so that she had an excuse to look right into them.

Easy's mouth dropped open. "You're kidding me?"

Jenny shrugged. "I'm from New York. I think I took a pony ride at a street fair once. A woman led me around in a circle. I don't know if that counts." Jenny cocked her head and grinned. "Actually, it might have been a donkey."

Easy laughed. "There's a pretty big difference." He ran his hand through his hair, making his curls even more disheveled than usual. He looked at Jenny shyly. "Well, you can always come with me sometime. If you wanted." He shrugged, like he wasn't sure if she'd be interested. "Credo's very gentle with beginners."

Jenny concentrated on the charcoal-scrawled eyes on her paper instead of the ones on Easy's face. Why was he *doing* this to her? "I'd like to . . ." She took a deep breath and looked up at him, lowering her voice a little so that everyone wouldn't hear. "But, um, what's going on with you and Callie? Are you together or not? Because . . ." She trailed off.

Easy looked surprised and flustered. "No, Callie and I aren't really . . ." He paused, not knowing what they were. He picked up his kneaded eraser and started to play with it like it was Silly Putty, stretching it until it broke, then rolling it back together. "I think we both know that things are over. . . . It's just not, technically, official."

Jenny felt her chest tighten in a combination of excitement at the possibility of being with Easy and dread over Callie finding out. "I just don't think it's the greatest idea for us to be spending a lot of time together before you guys are, you know, official," Jenny surprised herself by saying. She even kept drawing as they talked, capturing the way his eyes crinkled when he was trying not to smile. "She's my roommate, and I don't want things to get weird." *Weirder than they are,* she added silently.

"Hey, I totally understand." Easy reached across their desks and pulled down the top of Jenny's sketch pad so that she would look at him. "I didn't mean to cause any problems for you."

She lightly sketched in the loose curls that framed Easy's face. "I know." She noticed something stuck in his hair, and without thinking twice about it, she leaned across the desks toward him, making sure her boobs didn't touch her paper and smear her drawings. He leaned toward her a little, and Jenny was sure she was blushing as she pulled a piece of leaf from one of his thick dark curls. She held it up for him to see.

"I wondered what you were doing," Easy said, sounding a little disappointed, like he thought she was . . . what? Going to kiss him? Goose bumps covered Jenny's bare arms, even though the art building was always a thousand degrees because of the kilns. "I was out in the woods this morning," he said mysteriously.

"Really? How come?" She loved the idea that Easy was sort of a wild boy, like a woodland sprite or something, only not the gay tights-wearing kind. Jenny glanced up at the sound of the door closing. She'd kind of forgotten where she was. Kids were headed outside, armed with their sketches, to spray them with fixative. Class was almost over already? How did that happen? She looked down at her table and saw that she'd drawn a whole stack of sketches of Easy.

"I like to paint there. It's quiet. I've got this great spot." Easy yawned and stretched, glancing around the art room as the students started to move their drawing desks back to their original places, the metal feet squeaking across the wood floor. "I was going to go there again tomorrow. Maybe you'd like to come?" Easy's piercing blue eyes met Jenny's, and she tried to understand what he was asking. Tomorrow? Did that mean he would be breaking up with Callie—*today*? Suddenly it felt like everything was happening so fast. Was it too fast?

Not that she cared. "Yes. I'd like that."

To: EasyWalsh@waverly.edu
From: CallieVernon@waverly.edu
Date: Wednesday, September 11, 3:55 p.m.
Subject: Re: Stables

Did you get my last email? See you at 5!

Kisses and maybe more . . .

Xxx,

C

WAVERLY OWLS SHOULD AIR THEIR DIRTY LAUNDRY BEHIND CLOSED DOORS.

Easy stretched out on his bed and listened to the sounds of guys returning from sports practice, their adrenaline-pumped voices echoing through the dorm as they headed for the showers to get cleaned up for dinner. Alan, his roommate, was out having dinner at The Petit Coq with his parents, probably getting drunk with them on the red table wine. Easy turned the volume up on his iPod and let the sound of the White Stripes fill his ears. He was excused from mandatory team sports because of Credo, and he would have been out riding her this afternoon if he hadn't been avoiding Callie. He didn't know what it was that had changed between them exactly, but a year ago he hadn't been able to keep his hands off her. He would have jumped at the chance to spend some quality time before dinner snuggling in the privacy of the stables; now he couldn't even face answering her emails or messages. What the fuck was his problem? Why was he being such a shithead?

Because he'd met Jenny. Easy smiled to himself at the thought of her. It was inevitable that he'd tell Callie, but couldn't he put it off just a little longer?

The sound of high heels dinging up the dorm's marble stairs could be heard over the sound of Jack White's wicked guitar playing. "Damn," Easy murmured under his breath. It was time. He shut off the music.

The door flew open and there stood Callie, in all her fury, looking beautiful and slightly deranged, like a debutante scorned. "What are you *doing* here? Did you not get my messages?" Her left eyelid twitched a little, like it always did when Easy pissed her off enough. He tried not to smile. He still loved her. Always would. Especially when she was mad. "I skipped out of field hockey early so I could meet up with you, and you don't even bother to *show?*" Callie's hair was pulled back in a clip, and she had clearly taken time to clean up for him after practice. She looked a little too neat and polished in her short gray wool skirt, black tights, and black leather kitten-heel riding boots. As far as Easy knew, she had given up riding when she was seven, even though he had tried, many times, to get her on Credo. The smell of her shampoo reminded Easy of the salons where his mother and all her girlfriends spent entire afternoons getting their hair and faces molded into something completely unrecognizable.

"I'm sorry. I'm really sorry," he said lamely. He sat up, noticing how out of place Callie looked in his disaster of a room.

Crumpled boxer shorts and jeans covered the floor and a banana
peel lay on top of his eight-drawer dresser, level with Callie's face.

She saw it but ignored it. "That's all you can say? You're
sorry?" Callie pulled the clip out of her hair and shook her head
so that her strawberry blond locks fell in thick waves around her
shoulders, something that usually drove Easy wild. She gazed at
his familiar blue eyes, trying to figure out what was different
about them. Maybe the way he was looking back at her?

"Wait. You're sorry about blowing me off or . . ." Callie's
heart started to pound so hard it felt like it would break free of
her chest. Running from the stables to his dorm, she'd been furious, ready to punch Easy in his beautiful face but also ready to
accept his explanations or excuses, provided they came sweetly
enough, and with plenty of kisses to smooth it over. Now it
sounded like smoothing it over was the last thing on his mind.

"I can't do this anymore, Callie," he murmured softly at the
wall.

"You can't do *what*? Be with me?" She choked back a sob. She
was not going to cry. This was *not* over. "What are you *talking*
about?" If she could just find the right thing to say, she knew she
could make it better. In a few minutes they'd kiss and make up.

"You know things haven't been right with us," he faltered.
Fuck, what had he gotten himself into?

"That's not true. We're great together." She tossed her hair
over her shoulder and kept her voice light. "It's just—it's the
beginning of the year. Things are stressful. It'll get better, I
promise."

Easy shook his head slowly. Callie could tell he was trying not to look at her. "It's just not working," he said in a low voice, playing with the buttons on his iPod. "Don't pretend like you haven't noticed. If everything was great, you wouldn't have been making out with Heath fucking Ferro on Saturday."

"We were *not* making out," Callie protested, her mind whirring, already trying to decide on what tactic to take here. How much had he *really* seen? Maybe she should just play dumb. But part of her swelled with anger—yes, she'd been drunk and playing spin the bottle, but the *reason* she was drunk in the first place was because she was upset about Easy, so he should really be more understanding. "It was just a *game*."

Easy stared at her. "That's no excuse." He ran a single, paint-splattered hand through his messy curls.

"Easy, look, I know things have been rough, since, well, since Spain and everything." She thought back to the night in Spain when she'd told him she loved him and he had practically asked what they were having for dinner. "But we can *fix* it." Callie sat down next to him on the bed, put her hand on his knee, and tried to look as persuasive as possible. She stuck out her lower lip in the way that always made her stern father cave and give her whatever she wanted.

Easy sighed heavily, like he was about to say something he knew Callie wouldn't want to hear. *So don't say it,* Callie thought. "That's the thing," he began. "I don't want to fix it." He stared at her hand on his knee as if wishing it would go away. Then he looked straight at her, his blue eyes cold and serious.

She moved her hand and jumped abruptly to her feet. "This is about Jenny, isn't it?" she practically shouted.

"Not really," he replied slowly. "It's about us."

Not really? *Not really?* As in, *kind of?* "I cannot believe you are breaking up with me to go out with that little . . . that little . . . *pimple!*" Callie shrieked. "How dare you!"

"It's not like that, Callie." Easy kept his voice level and slow in response to her increasing hysteria. He knew this was going to get messy. Callie had a tendency to melt down like a five-year-old when she didn't want to face something.

Callie narrowed her hazel eyes at him. "So, are you, like, *into* her now?"

"Stop it." Easy pressed his fists to his temples. This wasn't part of his breaking-up-with-Callie conversation. Whatever his feelings were for Jenny, they didn't have anything to do with Callie. "This isn't about anyone but you and me."

Callie nodded violently. "Oh, sure. Of course not. Like eager little Jenny throwing herself all over you had nothing to do with it." She clenched her fists. "That *bitch!*"

Easy stood up. Talk about being a bitch. "How can you start flinging names at people like that? Do you even *remember* how you and I got together, or did you block that out?"

Easy saw from the way her face froze that it wasn't a good move to remind Callie how she'd dropped Brandon like a dead-weight to go out with him. He'd always been ashamed of the shady way they'd gotten together behind Brandon's back and in front of the rest of the Waverly population. At the time, he and Callie just had so much natural chemistry that it all seemed okay and even sort of romantic. But now, it was just another thing that bothered him about their relationship.

"You were certainly trying hard enough to get your hands up my skirt that night!" Callie screamed.

Easy tried to lower his voice, noticing, for the first time, that the door was still open. "I *know*." He shrugged, wishing he could just hug Callie and make it all okay. "I'm sorry I brought it up. We were both wrong. Let's just leave everyone else out of it, okay?" Fuck, this was why he hated confrontation. Everything became a jumble in his head and he ended up spitting out the things that were least important and forgetting about the things that counted. "I just don't think we work together anymore. We've changed. That's all."

Callie's whole body was shaking now, and Easy thought for a moment that she was about to start sobbing, which he couldn't take. Yeah, Callie had manipulated him and Jenny both. But he didn't . . . couldn't . . . hurt her. He just wished he could make her understand. But maybe that was asking too much since he didn't really understand it himself.

But instead of bursting into tears, Callie fluffed up her hair and turned her body toward the door. "Sure. Okay. *Fine.* I get it." Her voice was chirpy and mock cheerful now, like the children's activities director on the one cruise Easy's parents had ever been able to drag him on. "It's over. No problem."

Callie glanced over her shoulder and flashed Easy, the only boy she'd ever really loved, a withering smile. Holding her breath as she sprinted down the stairs, she dashed out of Richards before collapsing into tears on the grassy quad.

OwlNet   Instant Message Inbox

RyanReynolds: U hear that? Sounds like Walsh won't be getting any anymore.

TeagueWilliams: Callie's pissed he's getting TOO MUCH from the new chick with the boobs.

RyanReynolds: Oh yeah? Word.

OwlNet   Instant Message Inbox

EmilyJenkins: Just saw C walking across the quad with her makeup streaking down her face. What's up?

AlisonQuentin: EZ broke up with her.

EmilyJenkins: No way . . .

AlisonQuentin: Yup. For Jenny.

EmilyJenkins: Hello awkwardness in room 303!

HeathFerro:	Hey hot stuff, hear the latest juice?
TinsleyCarmichael:	I already heard about ur nickname, Pony.
HeathFerro:	No, funny girl. Easy just told Callie they're through. Got pretty nasty.
TinsleyCarmichael:	Fuck-a-doodle-doo. She OK?
HeathFerro:	U know Walsh ain't nothing special. I hear he's not that great anyway, though maybe u know the answer to that?
HeathFerro:	Hello?
HeathFerro:	Helllllllooooooo?

9

A WAVERLY OWL HELPS HER ROOMMATE WIPE HER NOSE NO MATTER HOW MESSY IT GETS.

Callie crossed the quad in a haze, knowing that she looked like something from a horror movie with her makeup running all over the place, but she was too distraught to care. She felt like her heart had been thrown out a two-hundredth-floor window to splat on the pavement below, so it seemed appropriate that she should look comparable. Even her perfect Façonnable wool skirt now seemed ridiculously short, and her Chloe kitten-heel riding boots, bought with the hope that they'd inspire Easy into some sort of sexy riding instructor fantasy, looked unbearably slutty.

She could feel everyone's eyes on her, but contrary to popular belief, she was not comfortable in the spotlight. One of Callie's mother's oft-repeated maxims was *Never let them see you cry.* Callie had been grateful to be sent to boarding school in the sixth grade, three years before her mother was even elected governor, if only to escape being reminded daily of the importance of proper posture and enunciation. Basically, Callie's parents had missed her entire adolescence, but she was probably better off because of it. She hated being home now, if that was what you called the thirty-plus-room Greek Revival mansion decorated entirely with museum-quality Federal period furnishings and lots of stuff that belonged to the state of Georgia and not them.

When Callie opened the door to room 303, Tinsley was sitting at her desk, her white iBook open and her fingers typing furiously, a pair of black plastic reading glasses bought in Milan perched on her perfect nose. "What's wrong? Is it Easy?" she demanded. She was barefoot, wearing black Parameter tuxedo pants and a cropped black Juicy Couture tee that showed off a slice of her concave stomach, her dark hair pulled back in a loose braid. She looked like a girl who would never in a million years get dumped—something Callie could no longer claim.

Callie burst into tears again. "He *dumped* me!" she wailed, still incredulous but already resigned to it. *I was dumped. I was dumped by Easy Walsh,* she repeated in her head, as if repetition could make it more comprehensible.

Callie could see from Tinsley's face that she was already prepared for disaster. Of course people were gossiping already. Easy probably had an underground fan club just waiting to spread the word the second he became single again.

"Why? Why would he do that?" Tinsley grabbed the box of tissues from her bedside and brought them to Callie. With Brett so caught up in her own life and her fancy love affair with Mr. Dalton, Tinsley was the only real friend Callie had.

"Because he doesn't like me anymore." Callie grabbed a tissue and blotted her face. "I don't know. Because he thinks I'm repulsive?"

"You *know* you're being ridiculous." Tinsley squeezed her shoulder with her French-manicured hand. "He could not find anyone more gorgeous than you if he spent the next fifty years searching. I can't *imagine* what he's thinking. He must be insane." She shook her head in disbelief, as if Easy breaking up with Callie was as incomprehensible to her as the latest practice SAT they'd all been assigned. It made Callie feel a teeny bit better.

"You're right," Callie agreed, mimicking Tinsley's sense of indignation. "What an asshole." It felt a little better to be angry instead of crushed. Screw Easy. Screw midget Jenny. Screw whatever the fuck was going on between them. She sat down on her bed and tugged off her heavy boots. They made her legs look too skinny anyway.

"We should make him pay for this," Tinsley said wickedly. Her violet eyes flashed as if she herself had been dumped. She'd always been one for plans, projects, and schemes, and the thought of plotting to avenge her brokenhearted friend made her tingle with excitement. Her parents had been madly, adorably in love for over twenty years, so she had an idea of what love should be, and she didn't like to see people abuse it.

"Right," Callie answered, hoping maybe Tinsley knew some sort of hex they could put on Easy to render him completely unattractive to women. Something that would make his dark curly hair start to grow all over his body until he looked like King Kong.

"You were way too good for him anyway. He smells like horses."

Callie groaned, and her hazel eyes filled with tears once again. She loved the way Easy smelled. It reminded her of when she was a kid and used to ride.

Tinsley lit a cigarette and handed it to her. "You need to take your mind off him. Think about other things."

"Easier said than done." She sucked smoke into her lungs. Tinsley sat on the bed behind Callie, Indian style. She did yoga daily and was the most flexible person Callie had ever met. Without even asking, she grabbed Callie's hairbrush from beside her bed and started to brush Callie's long, strawberry blond hair, something she'd always done last year. Tinsley was gentle, holding Callie's head in place with one hand while combing through her locks with the other. It was a sweet gesture, and Callie almost started to cry again. *Sweet* was not a word most people associated with Tinsley, but she could be incredibly tender when she wanted to be.

"I saw the guys coming out of the woods yesterday, all secrety-secrety about something." Tinsley changed the subject, working at a snarl at the back of Callie's neck.

Callie leaned her head back, loving the feel of someone else brushing her hair. It was so soothing, like getting a pedicure. "Like some sort of male-bonding thing?" she asked dreamily.

"Yeah, where they beat their chests and pretend they're animals and don't have calc homework to do." Tinsley was still a little bitter about being excluded from anything, and hanging out with the boys was always fun. Now she would just have to make her own fun. "Let's show them. Let's start our own club.

Except ours will be smarter and sexier." You could hear the excitement in her voice, and it was contagious. "We could have, like, a secret society."

"None of those jackasses allowed," Callie said firmly. It would be fun to get away from slimy boys for a while. "And no boyfriends allowed either. You know, I haven't been single in a long time— before Easy, it was Brandon. And before Brandon, it was . . ."

"Ethan Lasser!" Tinsley said in a nasal voice, mocking Ethan's Long Island accent. "Didn't he have to transfer to Deerfield when you broke up with him, he was so heartbroken?"

Callie laughed again and took another drag on her cigarette. She had to admit how great it was to have Tinsley back. Even if she looked like a fucking model, she knew how to make you laugh. "Well, I don't know if that's why he left. But I *did* break his heart."

"You know what you are? A serial dater. You *only* have long-term relationships, and you go from one to another without stopping to look around." Tinsley tossed the brush on the bed and patted Callie's head affectionately before lying down on her side. "You need to take a break. Get less serious for a while."

Easy for *her* to say. Tinsley grew bored with a guy after twenty consecutive minutes in his company. She didn't mean to—she was just a victim of little bursts of infatuation that ended as quickly as they began. But maybe she was right. Maybe it would be good for Callie to have a few one-night flings instead of long-term boyfriends. *"Boyfriend,"* Callie said slowly, as if trying to figure out the Latin root of the word. *"Boyfriend.* What a strange, ugly, totally un-fun word!"

"See? Boyfriends are such downers." Tinsley rolled onto her

back, her dark hair spreading around her head like a black halo. "You're always worrying about where they are, who they're with, what they're doing, blah blah blah!"

"Exactly!" Callie laughed, then sighed heavily. In fact, right now all she wanted to know was where jerk-face Easy Walsh was, and, more important, who he was with. "You're right."

"Good thing Brett's already shaken Jeremiah loose."

Callie hesitated for a minute, wondering if it would be wrong to mention Eric Dalton. She felt bad keeping something from Tinsley in the middle of all this sisterly camaraderie. "Well, she is sort of seeing someone. She hasn't mentioned it to you?"

"No." Tinsley was a little disappointed that Brett hadn't told her anything, but she didn't want to show it. "We haven't really had a chance to catch up yet." She pulled a tube of Guerlain KissKiss gloss in Rouge Passion from her pocket and applied it to her lips. "Who's she seeing?"

Callie let Tinsley suffer for a moment before answering in her Georgia drawl, slowly and dramatically, "Eric. *Dalton.*"

"You mean that's for *real*?" Tinsley jumped off the bed. So the rumors *were* true. Brett had snagged a teacher? A totally deliciously hot teacher. She would have imagined that *she'd* be the first one to hook up with a teacher, not Brett. Though to be fair, Brett was sort of the type a teacher would go for. With her radical red bob and multiple-pierced ear, Brett looked way more worldly and jaded than she was. Total overcompensation for being a completely innocent V-I-R-G-I-N. Brett claimed to have lost it in Sweden or Switzerland or something, but Tinsley saw right through that lie. "Are they *sleeping* together?"

"Nah." Callie thought briefly about how she had been ready to sleep with Easy, how she had been practically begging him for it and he just wasn't interested. But Brett hadn't come home last night and didn't explain herself, so she must have been with Mr. Dalton. Callie was sure she would have said something if they'd had sex, though. How could you keep quiet about *that*? "I don't think they've done it yet."

"Well, it looks like I'll get to check out her boyfriend up close tomorrow." Tinsley leaned back on her pillow, looking extremely pleased with herself. "He's my adviser."

"Lucky you." Callie could tell something was brewing inside Tinsley's mind. It was kind of a relief that Tinsley was on her side. At least for now.

OwlNet

EmilyJenkins: B, you in ur room?

BrettMesserschmidt: Nope. Hiding out in library. What's up?

EmilyJenkins: U like your roomie Jenny right?

BrettMesserschmidt: Yeah, she's cool.

EmilyJenkins: So then u want her to stay alive?

BrettMesserschmidt: What are you talking about now?

EmilyJenkins: Well . . . EZ just broke up with C and everyone heard her screaming about J.

BrettMesserschmidt: Where's Callie now?

EmilyJenkins: Back at Dumbarton I think.

BrettMesserschmidt: I should tell Jenny, huh?

EmilyJenkins: That's what I was getting at. . . .

BrettMesserschmidt: Fuck.

OwlNet

BrettMesserschmidt: Hey J, where are you?

JennyHumphrey: Checking email in the lab. How r u? How was last night . . . ?

BrettMesserschmidt: Good. Listen . . . Easy broke up with Callie.

JennyHumphrey: Um . . .

BrettMesserschmidt: Everyone's saying it was for u. Callie thinks so too.

JennyHumphrey: Jeepers.

BrettMesserschmidt: Yeah. So you might want to, like, sneak in after curfew . . .

JennyHumphrey: Thanks for telling me. You avoiding the room too?

BrettMesserschmidt: U could say that.

WAVERLY OWLS SHOULD FIND COMMON GROUND
WITH THEIR ADVISERS.

Thursday morning, Tinsley took her time walking to Stansfield Hall for her first meeting with her new adviser, the infamous Mr. Dalton. She hadn't taken any special care getting dressed this morning—it was easy to appear effortless when half your clothes are made specifically for you—and had unconsciously chosen a fairly chaste outfit. Her forties-style flutter-sleeved, white georgette blouse and chocolate Tocca pencil skirt with embroidered daisies seemed, at first glance, quite proper. Until you noticed the slit that showed off most of her perfectly slender thigh and the distracting way the lines of her red Blumarine bra could be seen through the delicate chiffon whenever she shifted a certain way, which she could be counted on to do. Even her purple suede peep-toe Miu Miu wedges implied repressed sexiness, which Tinsley knew was far more seductive than blatant sexiness.

Her father was a globe-trotting businessman, always involved in dozens of multinational ventures and investing in companies that drew him to places like Cape Town and Beijing and Oslo. Tinsley's mother was a photojournalist and former model, half Portuguese, half Danish, an ethnic combination that happened to be one of the world's most aesthetically pleasing and to which Tinsley's owed her unbelievable violet eyes. Her parents had treated her like an adult since she began to speak, so she'd always felt comfortable with an older crowd—they talked fast and moved faster, and that's how she liked to feel like she was living, at the fastest speed possible. Chiedo, their translator and guide over the summer, must have been twenty-five, though it never occurred to her to ask him. Eric Dalton, if he had just graduated from Brown, couldn't be much older than twenty-two. That was nothing.

After all, when she met him at Chapel, he had practically been drooling. Tinsley might have felt guilty if Brett had actually told her what was going on between them, but if Brett *thought* she didn't know and had no plans to tell her, Tinsley had every right to flirt with Mr. Dalton as much as she wanted to. So there.

She heard a Billie Holiday song playing from behind his closed office door. *The very thought of you and I forget to do . . . those ordinary things. . . .* She pictured him flipping through his CDs, trying to decide what would make the best sound track for their first official meeting. Billie Holiday was a bold choice—because she was such a jazz classic, it couldn't be construed as inappropriate in any way, yet her throaty, dramatic voice was so blatantly sexy, it had to reveal something about the inner workings of Mr. Dalton's brain. She hadn't even met him yet and she'd already read his mind.

Mr. Dalton opened the door and Tinsley was startled again by how beautiful he was. His hair was damp, which instantly conjured up images of him stepping out of the shower and reaching for a very small towel. He smelled like Polo aftershave, and Tinsley found herself longing to touch his smooth, freshly shaven cheek.

"Tinsley Carmichael. Very nice to see you again." His voice was deep and very professional, but this was quite clearly the highlight of his day. Where did he go from here? Trying to teach bored freshmen to care about Thucydides and Herodotus and all those other impossibly ancient historians? An intimate meeting with his gorgeous advisee was clearly the perfect way to start off his day.

"Hey, Mr. Dalton." She stepped inside his cluttered office, loving everything about it and him.

He groaned in mock anguish. "Eric, please." He indicated the leather chair in front of his desk, and Tinsley took a seat, smoothing her skirt and crossing her legs in one unified, elegant gesture. Eric pretended not to notice the slit in her skirt and sat down behind his desk. He shuffled through a stack of folders before pulling one out and opening it. "I've always felt like students should be able to call teachers by their first names. It makes them seem more human. And it makes me feel less ancient."

Tinsley had no trouble thinking of Eric as anything but human—a very healthy, red-blooded man human. Maybe she would have taken a greater interest in ancient history if Eric had been her teacher.

He smiled across the desk at her. "So, how have things been going for you since your return to Waverly?"

Vague question, she thought. What *things*? Classes? Boys? Annoying roommates? "Fine. It's nice to be back." As exciting as it was to travel the world with her parents, there was something reassuring about being back on Waverly turf, back where she knew how to spin teachers and toss off A papers on Nathaniel Hawthorne in under an hour and where the food wasn't so exotic it bordered on inedible.

He leaned toward her. "You know, as your adviser, I'm supposed to keep an eye on you, make sure things like the Ecstasy incident don't happen again." Eric looked stern for a moment, and Tinsley could tell he was getting a kick out of pretending to intimidate her.

She nodded humbly, trying to look repentant. "It won't."

"Good," Eric said, looking satisfied. "It's part of my job to make sure you stay on the right track."

"*The* right track?" Tinsley asked. "It seems like there should be more than one."

"For you, I'm sure there are," Eric said with a smile, revealing a toothpaste-white grin that reminded Tinsley of when she was eleven and used to practice kissing on an eight-by-ten photo of Ashton Kutcher. "What about colleges? Any thoughts?"

"Well, I'm looking into Columbia right now," Tinsley lied, hating to even think about college. When pressed, she said Columbia, but really, Columbia and Princeton and Amherst and Williams all seemed like bigger versions of Waverly—filled with jaded spoiled kids exactly like her.

"Columbia's a good school. And what about after college?" Eric smoothed his tie against his chest and glanced down at the open folder on his desk. "I see your grades are solid in all subjects—A-minuses or B-pluses. But . . . I guess I don't really get a good sense of where your interests lie." He looked up from his folder and met Tinsley's gaze for a little longer than appropriate. A chill ran down her spine—it felt like he was trying to peer inside her. "Besides varsity tennis since you were a freshman . . ." Eric raised his eyes from her folder to give Tinsley an appreciative eyebrow raise, as if to say he'd love to see her on the court sometime. "Your only extracurricular is Cinephiles, the film society."

"I actually *founded* the Cinephiles," Tinsley replied, a bit defensively.

"Well, *that's* impressive."

"It's not a big deal." Tinsley was modest now. "But there's this state-of-the-art screening room in the basement of Hopkins Hall that only gets used when a teacher decides to show her class a film." Tinsley shook her head. "Have you been down there yet?" The film room was one of the sexiest places on campus, with expensive leather reclining theater chairs, a fourteen-foot-wide screen, high-tech lighting, and surround sound. There were only about twenty seats, so it was intimate, like the kind of private screening room a Hollywood director might have in his Beverly Hills mansion.

"No, I haven't." Eric looked intrigued. "I didn't even know Waverly had something like that—they certainly didn't in my day."

"You should definitely check it out." She thought of how

exciting it would be to sit in the dark with Eric, watching something sexy and dramatic like *Body Heat* on the big screen. Or not
watching it. Out in the hall, some band geeks were discussing
which songs they needed to perfect for homecoming. Losers.

"You know what I think?" Eric asked, planting his elbows on
the desk. She could imagine a few things he must be thinking.
She shifted gracefully in her seat and refrained from playing with
her hair, a gesture she thought girls overused when trying to get
guys' attention, and instead concentrated on holding his gaze,
which was more difficult than she expected. His eyes seemed to
bore into her. "I think you are one of those very rare people who
have so many talents, they have a hard time deciding on the
right ones to use."

That was cryptic. What did that mean, the *right ones*? "I'm
not sure I know what that means," she said coolly, tugging her
skirt down over her knees.

"Nothing bad," he quickly assured her, flashing her an intimate smile. "Just that you're smart and good at everything you
do. I'm just trying to find out what turns you on."

Tinsley was suddenly encouraged. Without any prompting,
she spent the next ten minutes elaborating on her experience in
Cape Town and Johannesburg and the thrill of making a documentary in a country with such a shocking contrast of opulent
wealth and desperate poverty living right on top of each other
while it was still in the process of defining its post-apartheid
identity. The excitement of watching an entire nation try to
figure itself out inspired her and made her wish she could make
more documentaries, maybe even one about this messed-up

country of her own. It had been a high-intensity summer. She could feel her cheeks glow as she spoke, and she felt comfortable and excited. The words just tumbled out of her.

Eric nodded and jotted a few notes down on his pad. She noticed he had a few very faint freckles on the planes of his cheekbones.

Tinsley stopped talking abruptly. "Am I boring you?"

"Not a bit." Tinsley could imagine the two of them in a café in France, sipping their third espressos and unable to end their conversation. "Have you read the Fitzgerald story 'The Offshore Pirate'?"

Tinsley shook her head, her black hair gently swishing back and forth against her blouse.

"You remind me of the main character." His deep gray eyes glimmered, as if there was something else he wanted to say. Tinsley waited, but he didn't say it.

"Well, I hope that's a compliment." She laughed, already planning to head to the library between classes to check out the story. Being compared to a Fitzgerald heroine could be an insult, but she had a pretty good feeling that it wasn't. "Listen, I hate to leave, but I think I should be getting to class." She stood reluctantly.

"Anytime you need anything." Eric looked like he was trying hard to keep his face neutral. "You know where I am." He stood and moved toward the door, glancing at his Cartier tank watch on his right wrist. Next to it was a platinum-engraved gate-link bracelet. Without thinking, Tinsley reached out to touch it. Dalton seemed a little surprised by her sudden movement, but he didn't pull away.

"This is gorgeous," she said breathlessly, her fingertips tracing the delicate link design. "My father had one exactly like this that was stolen. Is it Victorian?" She looked up at him and realized his face was only about six inches from hers. She quickly turned back to the bracelet, fingering the latch and enjoying the closeness of his skin on her fingers. If she moved them a centimeter to the right, she'd be touching his arm. Her heart raced.

"I guess you know your antiques too." Eric gave her a quick smile and made no effort to step away. "Yes, um, it's Victorian. It was my great-grandfather's, actually, my great-great-grandfather's. It was a gift from the royal family for . . . I'm not sure what, actually." His chest rose and fell beneath his perfectly pressed shirt and tie. It was clear he was in agony, but Tinsley wasn't ready to let him get away yet. She looked up to find his cheeks flushed. She opened her violet eyes wider, knowing that from his angle, looking down at them through her thick black lashes, they were irresistible.

"Do you think I could borrow it?" This, she thought, was the ultimate test. If he gave it to her, it meant he was ready to forget all about Brett and take his chances with her. "I'd love to know what it feels like to wear it, just for a while."

Eric blinked his gray eyes. Without speaking or moving them from Tinsley's face, he unlatched the bracelet with his left hand and held it out to her. Instead of taking it, she thrust her right arm out, palm up, so that Eric could put it on himself.

"Be very, very careful with this," he told her solemnly as he fumbled with the latch, his fingers grazing her arm. "Your wrist is much smaller than mine, so keep your eye on it." Tinsley watched as his gaze progressed up her slender arm to her body.

"I will guard it with my life," she vowed, her lips unable to suppress a flirtatious victory smile. "And I'll give it back the next time I see you. I promise." Impulsively, she stood up on tiptoe, planning to kiss him on the cheek. He smelled like Ivory soap and Crest toothpaste. But just as her lips were about to touch his cheek, Eric turned his head, and her mouth landed halfway on his lips.

Oops, Tinsley thought happily. She kept her mouth where it was for a moment before finally pulling away. They stared at each other.

Eric spoke first, quietly, as if his voice were trying to hide some emotion. "Then I hope I'll see you again soon." He opened the door for her, keeping his eyes on her face the entire time. There were other students in the hall, hurrying off to class. Tinsley lingered outside his office as she fingered the bracelet.

"Don't worry, you will."

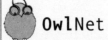

OwlNet Instant Message Inbox

EasyWalsh: Hey, how r u?

JennyHumphrey: Booooored. In a research seminar at the library. I already know how to use the dewey decimal system!

EasyWalsh: Bummer . . . Did you hear that it's, uh, official with Callie now?

JennyHumphrey: Yeah, I did . . . You okay?

EasyWalsh: Yup.

JennyHumphrey: That's good.

EasyWalsh: I really hope this doesn't sound sleazy, but do you want to meet up in the woods today for the art project we were talking about yesterday?

JennyHumphrey: OK.

EasyWalsh: I'll give you directions at lunch.

JennyHumphrey: Good. I'm . . .

EasyWalsh: Yeah . . . I think I know what you mean.

OwlNet   Instant Message Inbox

BrettMesserschmidt: Can I see you later?

BrettMesserschmidt: I've been thinking about you. . . .

[EricDalton has signed off Thursday, September 12, 10:37 A.M.]

A WAVERLY OWL DOES NOT POSE NUDE
ON A FIRST DATE.

Jenny could barely concentrate in English class on Wednesday, even though it was normally one of her favorites. She loved the way the classroom was set up as if it were a conference room—one giant oval table with fifteen chairs around it, filled with cashmere-sweater-wearing students and the ultra-petite Miss Rose, who wore bubble-gum-pink lipstick. It was a discussion class, which meant Miss Rose would talk for about ten minutes and then open the conversation up to the students. At first Jenny had been shocked at the intimacy and sophistication of it all. There was no hand-raising or wrong answers, just how she imagined classes would be in college. They were already a third of the way through *Madame Bovary,* and Jenny was completely enthralled with Emma and her struggles living with a man she didn't love. It made her wonder what it would be like to never find love or to be forced to settle for something inferior just because that's what people did. What would it be like to be stuck with a Charles Bovary when she knew there was an Easy Walsh out there?

"Jenny," Miss Rose said as the other students packed their bags and filed out of the classroom. "Is everything okay? You were awfully quiet today." Her hair was pulled back in a bun, making her look a little more severe than usual, but she still looked beautiful, like a china doll dressed in a black wool Dolce & Gabbana pantsuit. Whenever someone made some observation that was way off base, like maybe Emma Bovary was a lesbian, she'd say, "All right. What support for that can you find in the text?" instead of telling the student off. Jenny felt like she'd learned more from the *way* Miss Rose taught than the actual assignments in class.

"Oh, yes, I'm fine!" Jenny stuffed her notebook into her suede bag. It was packed with art supplies for her outing with Easy. The sight of her brand-new Rembrandt pastels and box of Prismacolor pencils sharpened and ready to go reminded her again that in twenty minutes, she'd be alone with the newly single Easy. "I'm just a little . . . distracted today."

Miss Rose nodded sympathetically. "Well, I really enjoyed your short paper comparing the imagery of the novel to the Realist painting style of Gustave Courbet. I thought it was fascinating that you made those connections. Congratulations!" She handed Jenny her paper back, with an enormous A+ on top. It was the first grade she'd received at Waverly. What a good omen for the day.

She nervously felt for the note Easy had slipped her at lunch.

Butterflies frolicked in her stomach. Jenny didn't exactly have a stellar track record in her romantic relationships. And there weren't many—her brief fling with beautiful stoner boy Nate had ended when she realized he was just using her to get back at his ex-girlfriend. Then there was her relationship with Leo, which had started out well, but she'd realized quickly that he bored her. Other than that, her romantic history included one molestation at the hands of creepy Chuck Bass and getting pawed at by Heath Ferro on the first day of school. She was so inexperienced with relationships, no *wonder* she was nervous.

In the dining hall at lunchtime, Easy had flashed her a smile and dropped a folded piece of paper on her tray. She'd forced herself to pick up a tuna fish sandwich and make a salad at the salad bar. Then she sat down at an empty table off to the side, grateful that there were only assigned seats for formal dinners. She took a bite of her sandwich and unfolded the note.

Directions to the SECRET painting pasture. (Shhhhhhh . . .)
Cross main quad toward woods. Take path to boathouse.
Halfway to the river, there's a patch of birches on the right. Turn
into them (watch for low branches) and walk about twenty
yards. It opens into a small clearing. Keep going and you'll come
to a bigger clearing. I'll be there.

Walking across campus now with her brandless aviators bought at the street market in Union Square, Jenny tried to calm down and enjoy the gorgeous afternoon. She wasn't used to the damp dirt, cut grass, and drying leaves that greeted her every time she stepped outdoors. Even when you were so deep in Central Park you could imagine you weren't in New York City, it never smelled like this, and you could still hear horns from cabs on Central Park West. As Jenny approached the woods, the pleasant scents grew even stronger—pine, mingled with the freshwater smell of an unpolluted Hudson. She was grateful not to be riding the crosstown bus home from Constance Billard right now, as she would have a year ago, wearing her ugly school uniform.

When she saw the thatch of birches, the butterflies started up again, but she plunged through the trees, careful to keep the clutching branches out of her curls. She felt like she was stepping out of civilization and into a private world, one inhabited only by Easy. And now her. She crossed the small clearing Easy had mentioned, noticing a Zippo lighter near a collection of rocks. This obviously wasn't the secret spot he was talking about.

She continued through the trees as they got closer together and any trace of a path disappeared. She was a little worried about getting lost—she'd never been a Girl Scout—before she caught a whiff of turpentine in the pine-scented air and knew Easy couldn't be far away. The trees abruptly gave way to a much larger grassy clearing, but she didn't see him at first. This had to be it, she thought, setting her bag down on a rock and admiring the beauty of her surroundings. The grass was the scratchy, wild kind, and tall stalks of purple asters and black-eyed Susans grew along the edge of the woods. She stepped closer to a giant rock just as Easy stood up from behind it and Jenny's heart skipped a beat, something she thought people just talked about happening. The sight of Easy, in his Levi's and a baby-blue T-shirt that said FOOD NOT

BOMBS, gave her such a thrill that her heart really did forget to beat.

Easy's face broke into a grin. "I like your T-shirt," Jenny told him shyly, her long brown curls tickling the tops of her arms. "My dad has a button that says that."

Easy looked down at his shirt, as if to remind himself of what he was wearing. "My father hates this shirt. He calls me a hippie when he sees it." He had put together his easel and was setting out his tubes of paint, brushes, bottles of oil and turpentine, and a paint-stained cloth.

Jenny stepped closer to him and started pulling her own supplies out of her bag, placing them on one of the large, moss-dappled rocks. "Well, my dad *is* kind of a hippie, so I know he'd approve."

"You're lucky." He didn't say anything else, and Jenny assumed he didn't get along too well with his father. But she didn't want to press it. Instead, he grinned at her. "Glad you found me."

"It's beautiful," Jenny said, meaning it. "I can see why you like coming here to paint. It's so peaceful."

"Yeah, it's great." Easy stretched his arms above his head, his T-shirt raising a little so that Jenny could see the top of his Calvin Klein boxers peeking out from his jeans. "So, did you look through the art syllabus yet?"

"Syllabus?" Jenny had no idea there even was a syllabus for art.

"Yeah," Easy teased. "You know, those things the teachers hand out at the first class?"

"Yes, smarty-pants, I know what a syllabus is." She stuck her tongue out at him. "I just don't remember getting one for art."

"Well, the midterm project involves incorporating portraiture into the landscape. Any media we want, any subject, any setting." He looked at Jenny sheepishly. "I knew right away what setting I wanted"—he indicated the field around him—"and I was hoping you'd be my subject."

Jenny had to keep her jaw from dropping. Easy wanted to paint her? Here? "You didn't tell me that's why you wanted me to come out here! I thought we'd both be . . . um, working."

"Oh, you can work too," he said with a smile. "You can talk or draw as long as you don't move too much," he said, repeating her words to him in art class. "I didn't get a chance to draw you in class, remember?"

"I can't believe you're working on your midterm project already!"

"I know." Easy's dark blue eyes searched her brown ones. "I'm not normally an overachiever, by any standards. But the wildflowers will be gone soon, so it seemed like the perfect chance. I've always wanted to paint someone here. . . ." He trailed off after that, looking suddenly nervous.

Always wanted to, Jenny thought. Meaning, *never had.* He'd never painted Callie here? Wow. It was as if he'd been waiting for her. Jenny could barely believe this was possible.

"I don't have to be naked, do I?" Jenny asked suddenly, and immediately regretted it. Her cheeks burned. "I—I'm not sure I'm ready for the entire art class to see me naked yet," Jenny stammered. "Even in a painting." Never mind the art class; she couldn't imagine what Easy would do with her boobs. He'd run out of paint!

Easy frowned in mock disappointment. "Clothes are okay."

Jenny looked around awkwardly. "Should I pose or something?" She fiddled with her necklace, a silver magnolia leaf on a leather cord wound twice around her neck, suddenly aware that the leaf looked like an arrow pointing directly downward toward her ample cleavage. As if Easy needed any signs to point him there.

He stepped toward her and clasped his chin in thought. "I was thinking Klimt by way of Modigliani, if that makes sense to you? On the grass, if it's not wet and you don't mind. Somewhere with wildflowers. I know it sounds totally cheesy, but I think I can make it work if I don't use too much pink."

Jenny thought she was more likely to be compared to the full-figured girls in a Rubens than the elongated figures of Modigliani, but let Easy see her however he wanted to. It was just so nice that he knew about art. Nate had posed for a series of portraits that she'd ultimately destroyed, but he'd just looked back at her vacantly with his blank stoner stare whenever she mentioned anything about art. If it didn't involve a bong or boobs, he definitely wasn't interested.

Jenny glanced around. It was a beautiful sunny day, the ground was dry, the sun was warm, leaves were rustling. Easy led her to a flat area of the pasture, and she spread out on her side, her sketchbook in front of her. Easy gave her his iPod, and she scanned through the songs. They both had Nirvana and a fair share of Bob Dylan, but he had more Lucinda Williams and

Emmy Lou Harris where she had Weezer and the Lemonheads. She picked an artist she hadn't heard before and took out her pastels. The sun beat down on her, warming her face and undoubtedly making her freckles spread, but she didn't care. She closed her eyes and let the late-summer sunshine bleed through her eyelids, wondering if, years later, she would be telling her children about this moment, in the woods with Easy, how this was the start of it all. The way their parents met.

She felt a hand on her shoulder. "Hey, sleepy." Easy shook her gently. Her eyes opened to see him kneeling beside her. He had a smear of yellow paint on his nose. Jenny laughed, hoping she hadn't dozed off long enough to have nap breath.

"I can't believe I fell asleep. I didn't snore or anything, did I?" she asked, sitting up. He stood and reached out a hand to pull her to her feet. She tried to memorize the feel of his warm fingers wrapped around hers. Even standing, Easy towered over her. He made her feel tiny.

"No." He grinned and pulled her toward the easel. "But you were talking in your sleep."

She gasped, knowing that her brother, Dan, would often pound on her bedroom door at night because she'd been babbling in her sleep. "You're joking! What'd I say?"

Easy scratched his head and pretended to look embarrassed. "You were kind of mumbling, so I couldn't really be sure . . . but it sounded sort of like . . . 'Easy Walsh, you're my hero.'"

God, he was so cute. "Very funny. But I usually only talk about movie stars in my sleep."

"Now that you mention it, you did say something about me reminding you of Jake Gyllenhaal."

Jenny laughed, realizing they were still holding hands. The air smelled like turpentine and Ivory soap and flowers. He smiled at her and she looked at his ever-so-slightly, adorably crooked teeth. His face was so close to hers, if she just . . . leaned . . . in . . .

"Let's see the painting." Her voice was overly bright to drown out the noise of her pounding heart. She'd had a million fantasies about kissing Easy, but he'd just broken up with Callie *yesterday.* The amazing thing was that he seemed to understand. "It's really just a basic sketch, so don't be too disappointed or anything."

When she looked at the canvas, she wouldn't have recognized herself. It was a close-up of a girl, stretched out in the sunny grass with wildflowers surrounding her, exactly as she must have looked the past two hours. A sketchbook open in front of her, the telltale white earphones of an iPod, the same white shirt and jeans and pink shoes, her head leaning on her arm, the cascading chestnut curls. But the face—it was the most finished part of the painting, but it couldn't be her. Perfect porcelain skin, rosy cheekbones, slightly open mouth, sleepy eyes covered with thick, lush lashes—it was very dreamlike and surreal, as if Easy had known what Jenny *wished* she looked like. Was it possible that he actually saw her that way? The whole painting, even only half finished, seemed to capture what it had felt like, lying there and listening to Easy's music, enjoying this secret, private space with him as if it were the only place on earth. Easy must have felt that way too.

"Wow," she said finally.

"Just wait till it's finished," he said a little dreamily. They packed up their things slowly. Easy held the branches back for Jenny as they made their way through the woods. Once they emerged, they walked side by side down the path back toward the quad, their legs brushing against each other comfortably as Easy held up the large canvas by its wooden stretcher boards.

That's when they saw Tinsley crossing the quad in front of them, dressed all in black and carrying a tiny red suede Marni handbag. Jenny immediately took a step away from Easy and felt like she was caught, even though Tinsley didn't appear to notice them coming from the boathouse path.

"It's okay," Easy whispered. "She's not going to bite. She didn't even see us."

But Jenny wasn't so sure about either of those things.

To: TinsleyCarmichael@waverly.edu;
BrettMesserschmidt@waverly.edu
From: CallieVernon@waverly.edu
Date: Thursday, September 12, 3:25 p.m.
Subject: URGENT

Hello ladies,

It's a beautiful day—waaaaay too gorgeous to go to practice. Better idea:
let's spend the afternoon at the Waverly Inn bar sipping G & Ts and not
mentioning a certain boy whose name starts with that cursed letter E and
who S-U-C-K-S.

Bring your fake ID and look sophisticated. The bartender's ancient, so
put on your best perverted smile and we'll be safe.

And what's with the midnight sneak-ins? I know you too well, Brett
Lenore Messerschmidt, and I'm calling your bluff. Forced BFF threesome
bonding will commence at 4 p.m. C u there . . .

Xoxo,

C

To: JennyHumphrey@Waverly.edu
From: EasyWalsh@Waverly.edu
Date: Thursday, September 12, 4:16 p.m.
Subject: Sunday?

Hey,

Thanks for letting me paint you today. I had a genuinely, seriously excellent time.

Maybe you'd want to come meet Credo on Sunday?

Hope so . . .

Easy

12

A WAVERLY OWL KNOWS TO LOOK AS MATURE
AS SHE ACTS. AND VICE VERSA.

The Waverly Inn was a short hike from campus, and Brett regretted wearing her green snakeskin Kate Spade pointy-toed pumps that looked sexy and sophisticated but pinched her feet. In her brand-new Marc by Marc Jacobs black satin pencil skirt and ultra-feminine Catherine Malandrino shell-pink bell-sleeved blouse, Brett felt surprisingly glad to be on her way to a "forced threesome BFF bonding" no matter how fucked up it sounded. In her mind, she vowed to be nicer to Tinsley. After all, Tinsley *had* saved their asses by taking the blame for the E incident and had spent the whole summer thinking she was expelled—even if she probably hung out with hot South African guys the whole time—and she'd been totally displaced by Jenny. But Brett hadn't heard any rumblings about her being a giant Jersey girl liar, so maybe she should cut Tinsley a break.

She stepped into the Waverly Inn lobby, headed past the dusty grand piano and straight into the bar. The hotel was the closest one to campus, where parents most often stayed, and its look of shabby opulence seemed befitting to the school. The bar had clearly passed its golden age and settled into a period of slow, decadent decline. It was nearly empty except for Tinsley and Callie, already seated at a wooden booth in the corner with three drinks in front of them.

"Your amaretto sour," Tinsley greeted Brett, indicating the one drink that wasn't half empty.

Brett slid in next to Callie, looking like a film producer or gallery owner in her emerald silk shell and a cropped Theory cardigan with a single mother-of-pearl button directly beneath her breasts, her wavy blond hair held back from her face by a pair of vintage gold barrettes. She would have looked very pretty, but her face seemed a little haggard, like she hadn't been getting her requisite ten hours of beauty sleep.

"You guys are awesome." Brett grabbed the glass and took a small sip. Strong, just the way she liked it, but it still made her wince as she swallowed. Tinsley was wearing a plain short-sleeve black T-shirt and jeans, but with her red lips (Guerlain KissKiss lipstick, as always), she had the air of a movie star sneaking out for a quick drink under the paparazzi's radar.

Brett leaned back against the wooden bench and looked at the framed nineteenth-century Currier-and-Ives-type ink draw-ings of the Waverly campus. "It's been too long since we've been here. I kind of missed it."

"It doesn't look like they've dusted since we were last here either." Callie sniffed the musty air. "But beggars can't be choosers." She took another big sip of her drink, and Brett noticed that her glass was already empty. Wow. She *was* taking the breakup with Easy pretty hard.

"How was your day, Callie?" Brett asked awkwardly, and Callie stiffened, like she could tell Brett was feeling sorry for her.

"It was fine. You know, I'm going to survive. But I just . . . don't want to talk about Easy for a while, okay?" Callie looked plaintively at her friends and twirled a blond lock around her finger. "Let's talk about other things."

"Other boys, you mean?" Tinsley chimed in, polishing off her drink. "You get started without me. I'll get another round." She slid out of the booth.

Brett was still nursing her first drink and already feeling a little light-headed.

"How's the D-man?" Callie suddenly asked.

"The D-man?" Brett repeated. "Come on, that makes him sound like a bad DJ or a pervert who only likes large-breasted women."

"Does he?" Callie put her elbows on the table and leaned forward. "Only like large-breasted women?"

"Apparently not." Brett stuck out her own barely B-size chest. "He seems to think these are all right."

"How well has he gotten to know them?" Callie giggled, then sucked at her skinny cocktail straw, making the ice cubes rattle around her empty glass.

"They're acquaintances, I'd say." Brett toyed with her gold earrings. The first half of her drink had gone straight to her head, and she was starting to feel a little more vocal than usual. *This is how you get yourself into trouble,* she thought. For some reason she was reminded of the night freshman year when she and Callie and Tinsley had bought graham crackers and Hershey's chocolates and marshmallows and sneaked over to the field house. Behind it was a giant charcoal grill that was used sometimes at pep rallies and Waverly picnics. Somehow they had managed to fire it up, and the three of them had toasted marshmallows and made gooey s'mores and drunk a bottle of red wine. Everything tasted so much better because the rest of campus was asleep.

Brett felt a burst of warmth toward Callie and was about to say something more about Eric when Tinsley reappeared with the grandfatherly bartender in tow, carrying a tray with three champagne flutes and a bottle of Moët & Chandon.

"What's this for?" Callie squealed with delight. She *loved* champagne. It was the only thing that made weddings and debutante balls bearable.

After the bartender left, Tinsley said, "My treat. I thought we could toast to our first all-girl outing and to the advent of the secret society!" Callie felt the men at the bar staring at them, trying to hear what they were saying. But instead of creeping her out, it made her feel sexy and bold. She could use some male attention right now, even from leering middle-aged alcoholics. "Cheers!" Callie raised her glass and clinked it against Brett's. *Take that, Easy,* she thought as she took her first sip. Then she downed it in order to stop talking to him in her head.

"So," Brett said with a giggle in her voice, the champagne clearly having the desired effect. "What does a secret society *do,* exactly?"

"I just think it's a good idea for girls to get together and talk and do things that make us feel sexy and bad," Tinsley offered.

"Like some kind of girl power thing?" Callie asked skeptically. "Will we have to burn our bras? Because I don't really need mine anyway." She giggled, indicating her almost-flat chest.

"I get what Tinsley means," Brett said, surprising Callie. Despite her suggestion they return to normal BFF behavior, she'd thought the tension between the two of them was there to stay. "Brianna says that whenever she breaks up with a guy, she has such a strong support system from her friends that it almost doesn't matter. " Brianna was Brett's cool older sister, the one who worked for *Elle* magazine and whom Callie was always trying to suck up to, just in case one day Brianna needed to get rid of all the incredible designer clothes in the magazine's fashion closet. It could happen.

"What about calling it Café Society?" Callie asked. "Doesn't that make it sound like a bunch of girls sitting around drinking and sharing sexcapade stories and advice and complaining together? But, like, in Paris, in the twenties?"

Tinsley and Brett grinned drunkenly at each other, and Callie definitely felt the ice between them melting. *See how great this girl power thing is?* she thought, her head beginning to feel quite pleasant and only a little fuzzy.

"I like it," Tinsley said. "We could dress the part—and come here or have mini-salons in our room! Without any of the guys around to bug us." She tossed her hair and grinned contagiously.

"Funny how just talking about sex makes you feel sexier, doesn't it?" Brett said.

"Tell us about your sexcapades this summer, Tinsley. You must have exciting news to report." Callie shifted toward Tinsley. She'd been dying to hear about Tinsley's conquests since the moment she reappeared out of nowhere. "Where'd you get the shark tooth?"

"Oh, Chiedo," Tinsley responded dreamily. "He was our guide in South Africa." She leaned back in the booth and closed her eyes, looking very dramatic. "You wouldn't *believe* how sexy he was. He was all muscle, and every time he touched me or even just looked at me, I felt like I was going to explode. He just made me feel so . . . wild and unrepressed." She shivered, as if just the memory of him gave her chills. "He was the second one." She opened one lovely violet eye to gauge their reaction.

"The second!" Callie heard herself gasp. She hadn't even managed to hook up with Easy this summer and he was her *boyfriend*.

"Before I met Chiedo, I had this little fling with a Dutch college student in Cape Town. He looked kind of like Derek Jeter but younger and with an accent. But he was nothing compared to Chiedo."

Brett rubbed her hands together. Even though Tinsley hadn't exactly *said* she'd had sex with them, Brett could only assume. She couldn't help wondering what was with her, taking so long to lose her virginity, when Tinsley could do it with two unbearably hot older guys over the course of one summer. If she couldn't do it with Eric, who *could* she do it with?

"Easy and I never did it. Is that weird?" Callie asked abruptly.

"No," Brett said, at the same time Tinsley said, "Yes." This struck them all as hilarious.

"What about you, B.? If you're not with Jeremiah, who are you working on?" Tinsley arched one of her dark eyebrows.

Brett felt her pale face coloring, and she cleared her throat. "You know, I'm sort of taking time off from boys for a while. It gets to be too distracting."

"What, are you into girls now?" Tinsley leaned across the table, her eyes flashing with intensity. "Or *men?*"

Brett looked her in the eye. "We'll have to see, I guess." She had no doubt that if Tinsley found out about her and Eric, she'd find some cute way to drop the bomb in front of the boys, or the entire dining room, or Dean Marymount. Tinsley was famous for subtly causing the equivalent of a gossip tsunami. "Anyway, I thought Café Society rules said no boyfriends."

"Boyfriends are different from men," Tinsley said with a yawn, arching her back and stretching like a cat. "Men are encouraged."

"Why don't we go get some pizza?" Callie interrupted. "I'm starved." Something about Callie, whose recent skinniness pointed to a larger problem, saying she was starving immediately placated the two other girls and set them into motion.

"Of course," Tinsley said, finishing her glass of champagne and setting it delicately on the slightly sticky table. "Let's go."

"Colonial?" Brett said. "Or Ritoli's?" She could definitely use something to soak up the liquor in her stomach, and both pizza places were right in town.

"Ritoli's has more *ambiance,*" Tinsley suggested, clearly referring to the Italian boys who worked there. It was a family-run business that had been in downtown Rhinecliff forever and was a favorite with the female population of Waverly. There were at least three young men working at all times, all dark and muscled and adorable.

"Stupid question," Brett said, and the three girls giggled and shuffled out of the hotel, leaving a generous tip for the bartender at their table.

Brett didn't realize how starved she was until they walked into Ritoli's and the warm rush of doughy air surrounded them.

"Mmmm," Tinsley said, rubbing her stomach. Then she elbowed Brett in the side at the sight of the handsome boy making his way toward them with menus.

"What do you guys want on it?" Tinsley asked.

"How about him?" Callie whispered a little too loudly.

Smooth, Brett thought.

"You want to look at the menus or you know what you want?" the boy asked, giving them all a knowing grin. He looked about seventeen, with dark eyes and smooth olive skin and the longest lashes Brett had ever seen. He even made her forget about Eric Dalton for a few seconds.

"Three Diet Cokes," Tinsley said, giving him her million-watt smile. "But we haven't decided what else yet."

"No problem. I'll be back in a few minutes."

It was warm inside, and Brett fanned her face with the menu and remembered how last year, after the first big lacrosse game, she and Jeremiah had met Easy and Callie and Tinsley and Heath here for pizza. They had to order another one because the guys devoured the first so quickly. She and Eric would never be able to hang out with her friends like that, she thought a little sadly.

But they had something different—it didn't have to be about eating pizza while the boys tried to flick a pepperoni into each other's spiked drinks. This would be her first real love affair, with much more at stake. Tinsley and Callie chattered on about the rumor that the entire pizza family was extremely well endowed and whether or not they could prove it. Their waiter came back, and Tinsley put in an order for a deep-dish pie with extra cheese and mushrooms on half.

"Earth to Brett." Tinsley waved her slender arm in front of Brett's face. "Anybody home?"

Brett didn't answer. Her eyes were fixed on the platinum link bracelet on Tinsley's right wrist. She stared. Was that . . . *Eric's*? It looked exactly like the one she had noticed him wearing when they went to Newport. The one from his great-great-grandfather. How on earth could Tinsley have it?

"That's a cool bracelet," Brett remarked, trying to keep her voice an alto although it sprang up to soprano in panic. "Where'd you get it?"

"Oh, my crazy aunt Elinore gave it to me the last time I saw her," Tinsley answered, twisting her wrist to admire the bracelet. "She's getting a little batty and gives away her shit whenever someone comes into her house. I walked off with this great pearl-drop necklace too."

Huh. How likely was it that two incredibly rare and valuable platinum antique bracelets that looked exactly alike would appear in the teeny town of Rhinecliff?

Pretty unlikely.

OwlNet

To: EricDalton@waverly.edu
From: TinsleyCarmichael@waverly.edu
Date: Thursday, September 12, 9:43 p.m.
Subject: Flappers and Philosophers

Eric,

It was such a pleasure meeting you this morning; consequently, I read the short story you suggested. I have a sinfully thin flapper dress that's exactly like something a Fitzgerald heroine would wear. . . . Thought you might enjoy seeing me in it sometime.

Much as I love being back at good old Waverly, sometimes I ache to feel the city pavement pounding beneath my heels again. Ever get the urge to disappear and hole up in a luxurious hotel suite, lounging in bed all afternoon and ordering Dom 1958 from room service? Thought daydreaming might be another thing we have in common . . .

T

BrettMesserschmidt: I just finished a bottle of Moët and you know what? I think we've gone slow enough. When do I get to see you next?

EricDalton: Brett, I've been thinking. . . .

BrettMesserschmidt: Good things, I hope.

EricDalton: The thing is, I don't think this is a good idea anymore—it's not smart. I'm sorry.

BrettMesserschmidt: Excuse me???

EricDalton: Maybe we should do this face-to-face?

EricDalton: Brett, are you still there?

BrettMesserschmidt: Is there someone else?

EricDalton: Of course not. But we need to go back to a purely student-teacher relationship, OK?

EricDalton: Hello?

EricDalton: Brett?

BrettMesserschmidt: Yes, sir. I think I understand. Perfectly.

A CLEVER WAVERLY OWL KNOWS HOW TO TELL
FRIEND FROM FOE.

"I didn't take the picture, did I? How is this possibly my fault?" Callie screeched into her cell phone, already tired of having to deal with yet another complaint from Nicholson Adams, her mother's publicist. Apparently a photo taken of Callie at a late-summer pool party had shown up in the Weekend section of the *Atlanta Journal-Constitution*, with the snide caption *Mary-Kate Olsen, Nicole Richie, and Governor Vernon's Daughter: Starving for Attention?* So what if she'd lost some weight in Barcelona, pining over the disaster that was her relationship with Easy? Who the hell's business was it, anyway? Not the *Journal-Constitution*'s and certainly not smarmy Nicholson Adams's.

Callie stood in the empty room in her camisole and Hanky Panky low-rise boy shorts, the phone having rung when she was about to put on her pajamas. As Nicholson proceeded to lecture her on how an eating disorder would reflect badly on constituents' views of her mother's family values, she looked at herself in the mirror. She turned to take in her thin body from a variety of angles, but nowhere did she see anything resembling the pin-thin bodies plastered in all the magazines. She certainly wasn't anorexic or anything—she'd just scarfed down three pieces of gooey Ritoli's pizza and half a bottle of champagne.

"Is my mother concerned that her daughter has an eating disorder or that people *think* her daughter has an eating disorder? If she's actually concerned about *me*, tell her that next time she can call herself."

She was about to hang up when he said, "Just try to eat something every once in a while, okay?"

"Eat this!" she screamed before hanging up. Then Brett walked through the door, looking like she'd witnessed a car crash. She'd gone outside with her cell phone when Nicholson called.

Callie pulled on her red satin pajama bottoms. "What's the matter, sweetheart?" Her voice immediately softened, and she was surprised at how the word "sweetheart" came out of her mouth so effortlessly. In her post-Easy existence, she must be transferring her thwarted affections onto her friends.

"Eric just IMd me," Brett blurted, her voice full of disbelief. Her normally pale face was a ghostly white. "He . . . he doesn't think we should see each other anymore."

"What?" Callie grew cold. *Shit.* This sounded like Tinsley's doing. Had she really made a move on Mr. Dalton? *Already?* "Did he say why?"

"He said it wasn't 'smart.'" Brett shook her head slightly. "But two days ago he didn't care if it was smart or not when we were practically naked in his bed."

"Did something change that made him realize how much trouble he could get in?" Callie asked dubiously. "Maybe he bumped into Marymount and freaked?"

"Maybe." Brett bit her lip and looked like she was about to cry. "But I don't know. He didn't say anything about Marymount."

Callie wondered if Brett had any suspicions that this had something to do with Tinsley returning, but of course Callie wasn't about to say anything. God, why was everything a fucking secret this year? "Well, it was just an IM, right? How much could he say?"

Brett stared at Callie blankly. "But I felt . . . so close to him. We almost did . . . it." At this, Brett's knees seemed to collapse under her and she fell dramatically onto her bed. "And then I just told him that I wanted to finally do it for real. And he just wrote back, saying it was over. It makes me feel so . . . sick and . . . stupid. Like I was some silly kid and he lost his patience with me."

"So fuck him. He's a jerk anyway," Callie gushed vehemently. Of course she desperately wanted to cheer Brett up, but she also felt a tiny bit relieved not to be the only dumped girl in Dumbarton 303.

"Who's a jerk?" Tinsley demanded, standing in the open door with her BlackBerry sticking out of the kangaroo pocket of her cutoff sweatshirt.

No one answered right away, and just as it was about to become awkward, Callie lamely filled in with, "Nicholson, my mom's publicist." If Brett and Tinsley didn't settle their issues soon, she was going to flip out. "Fuck him, telling me I'm too skinny."

Tinsley smiled indulgently. She'd go ahead and pretend she believed that's what they were talking about if Brett found it so impossible to speak when she was in the room. Fine. Tinsley was tired of giving Brett space for her moods—she could go right ahead and kiss her ass. "You are awfully thin, Cal. Your clothes have been looking kind of baggy." Which was true.

Callie rolled her eyes and shot Brett a thanks-for-nothing glare when Tinsley was hanging up her towel, but Brett was lying on her bed with her taxi-yellow Kate Spade rubber rain loafers still on, a single yellow leaf stuck to the bottom of one, staring straight at the ceiling, clearly in her own depressed world. Callie wondered what could distract her and immediately thought of Café Society.

"Where's the fourth Musketeer?" Tinsley pointed at Jenny's cot.

Brett glanced up disinterestedly. "She's in Sage and Emily's room. They have a French test tomorrow."

Tinsley rolled her eyes and flicked on the black Harmon Kardon stereo that took up one of the window seats. Radiohead came blaring out of the surround-sound speakers, and Tinsley tweaked the volume a little before flopping down on her stomach next to Callie. Her short PJ Salvage pink polka-dot boxer shorts showed off her long, toned legs. "We have some important business to discuss, girlies. We need to come up with some guidelines for Café Society."

"Rules?" Brett asked, sitting up so that she could check out Tinsley's wrist again, but it was now bare. Convenient. Or was she just paranoid? Brett went to her dresser and pulled from the top drawer her favorite thing to sleep in—one of Jeremiah's oldest J.Crew button-downs that was as soft as a tissue and so faded you could barely see its blue stripes. She'd slept in it for so long that it would have been weird to return it to him after she broke up with him.

"More like objectives," Tinsley said, rolling onto her back and crossing her ankles. "Or goals, if you will."

Suddenly Brett felt like she was at a slumber party with her best friends back in sixth grade. She grabbed her bottle of Kiehl's Crème de Corps and perched on the end of Tinsley's bed. Her bare legs were shaved smooth in anticipation of an evening with Eric. So she'd wasted her time, but it was still nice to have freshly shaven legs.

"Number one. No boyfriends," Brett said, forcing a smile for Callie and Tinsley.

Tinsley noted Brett's sudden enthusiasm. "Exactly. It is very critical for our growth as young women not to be hampered by whiny, self-involved boyfriends who are just trying to cramp our style."

"Two," Callie chimed in, her face glowing with interest. "Alcohol should always be involved."

"Three." Tinsley parted her hair in the middle and smoothed down each half so that she looked like a hippie. "Society members are encouraged to hook up with random, pre-approved gorgeous guys in a non-boyfriend, purely-for-fun sort of way."

"What?" Brett suddenly wondered if this whole project was just another way for Tinsley to reassert her dominance over everyone. "I thought this was just *talking* about hooking up."

"What fun would that be?" Tinsley demanded. "But I'm definitely not talking about group sex or anything. Not yet, at least." She flashed her wicked smile, the one that made you wonder if she was serious about anything at all or if life was just one giant game to her.

Maybe that's why Tinsley never gets her heart broken, Brett thought. That, and a face that would put Helen of Troy to shame.

"So who are these gorgeous guys?" Callie asked, rubbing Dr. Hauschka chapstick on her lips and handing it to Brett.

"Whoever we want them to be." Tinsley spread her hands out as if to indicate that these gorgeous guys were right there in front of them, just waiting to be chosen.

"Parker DuBois," Callie suggested. "He's sexy." Callie liked to think of herself as a good matchmaker, having put together and dismantled many of Waverly's notorious couplings due to behind-the-scenes manipulations. And while she was certain Parker and Brett would get along beautifully—they were both arty and moody—Parker was so hot, Callie wouldn't mind getting her lips on him either.

"What about Charlie Soong?" Brett offered. Charlie was a junior from Taiwan who could often be seen with a guitar and was supposedly a Taiwanese pop star, though he didn't talk about it. The girls had Googled him once last year and discovered that there were hundreds of Web sites run by rabid teenage fans in Taiwan sharing gossip, photos, sightings, and wondering what his life was like at the private boarding school he attended in the States. It was very surreal. "He's got those great soccer legs, even if he sings a cappella."

"He's a possibility," Tinsley mused, wondering what a Taiwanese pop star would be like to kiss. Maybe they did it differently there. She stood up and walked over to the antique oak mirror to examine her eyebrows for errant hairs. One of Tinsley goals for herself—one she never would have shared with her adviser—was to make out with someone from every single country on earth. Or at least the ones she could get to without a parachute or a dogsled. And what about that really tall guy she'd seen coming out of the woods with Brandon and the other boys? Whatever his name was, he wouldn't be a freshman forever. He could go on the list.

"You know who has to be first? The pizza guy," Callie said eagerly, still thinking about his warm brown eyes and tousled dark hair. He'd always smell like fresh pizza, which would be even better than having to eat it. "Toss me my South of the Highway?" Callie asked Tinsley, who was standing close enough to Callie's dresser to grab her nail polish.

"Angelo," Tinsley said, handing the pale pink polish over. "Yes." The other girls stared at her, wondering how she knew his name. "I asked," she said simply. "Thought it might come in handy."

"Sounds like we're going to have a pizza party, then," Brett said, not wanting to sound like she was too immature for this sort of thing, though she was having doubts. How weird was it to hook up with someone you hardly even knew? She watched as Callie expertly reapplied the polish to the bitten-down nails on her left hand.

"Guess we'd better decide who we'd like to invite into Café Society since it shouldn't just be us," Tinsley observed.

"Jenny, of course," Brett replied, taking the polish from Callie when it was time to do her right-hand fingers. Since they'd skipped practice and then dinner, Brett hadn't seen Jenny since that morning, and she suddenly felt guilty for leaving her new friend out. Especially since she'd been the one to basically tell Jenny to avoid Callie and the room for a little while. Brett wondered if she was okay.

Tinsley rolled her eyes toward Callie and wrinkled her perfect nose. "But she's a sophomore."

"Yeah, but she's cool," Brett argued defensively. There was just something about Jenny—this sort of *warmth*—that made Brett miss her when she wasn't around.

"Is she?" Tinsley pretended to examine the white tips of her French-manicured fingernails. "I mean, I haven't really talked to her. What do you think, Cal?"

"Do you think there's something going on between her and Easy?" Callie asked hesitantly.

"We'd know about it, wouldn't we?" Brett responded logically, though she didn't really sound convinced. "I mean, she lives with us. Anyway, it would be cruel to leave her out of Café Society."

Callie shrugged. It was hard to know if Jenny was a serious threat. "What about Benny? She needs to be in on this too."

"And Celine, and Alison. And Emily?" Brett said.

"Ugh. Emily is so milquetoast. Let's leave her out." Tinsley made a face. "We should probably let Sage Francis in, even though she can be a bitch. She's kind of fun."

"What about Verena Arneval?" asked Callie. Verena was a senior from Buenos Aires whose mother was the producer of a beloved Argentine soap opera. She had a sexy accent and a super-short pixie haircut and always wore dresses and heels, like an old-fashioned film star. "She's cool," said Callie.

The three of them looked up at the sound of voices in the hallway. "See you in class," Jenny called as she opened the door to Dumbarton 303. She almost jumped when she saw her three roommates staring at her.

"Oh! Hey, guys . . ." Jenny glanced at Brett. "What's going on?" She stood in the doorway for a moment, worried she'd walked in on something private. She stuck her hands into the pockets of her Citizens of Humanity wool cardigan. "Am I interrupting something? 'Cause I can go brush my teeth or . . ."

"No, come on in," Brett said, patting the bed next to her. "You're definitely included in this." Brett shot a glance at Tinsley, and the two of them held each other's gaze for a long, awkward moment. Jenny pretended not to notice and sank down on Brett's bed.

"Yes," Tinsley began after a long pause. "We're starting up our own secret society. And we wanted to extend the invitation to you." She flashed Jenny a generous smile, and Jenny's heart thumped. Tinsley wanted to include her? Jenny had to suppress an urge to jump up and hug everyone in the room—she was *in*! Of course, she knew that wouldn't be the coolest thing to do, so she managed to restrain herself, though she couldn't resist rubbing her hands together in excitement.

"A secret society?" she asked giddily. "That sounds like so much fun."

"That's the idea." Tinsley tossed her long, dark hair over her shoulders and leaned back against the pillows on her bed. *Like Cleopatra*, Jenny thought. "But we did want to talk about something with you first."

Jenny's stomach dropped. Of course it couldn't be that easy. She should have known there would be a hitch, like Tinsley wanted her to be the society's *janitor* or something.

Callie hopped up abruptly and headed to her dresser. She picked up her boar bristle brush and started to brush her hair, but Jenny could tell she was watching her in the mirror.

"We all know how dangerous rumors can be," Tinsley continued. "How they can end up hurting everyone involved. And I just feel—and I'm sure you agree—that we should probably clear the air about one rumor in particular." Tinsley paused for dramatic effect and smiled at Brett and Jenny. "Jenny, I know that Callie asked you to flirt with Easy so that she wouldn't get busted for having him in this room. And it was very nice of you to oblige and help keep Callie out of trouble." Tinsley glanced at Callie. "But the thing is, it's all over now—no one got in trouble. Yet I'm still sort of hearing things about you and Easy." Tinsley pursed her lips and stared directly at Jenny. "Is there anything we should know?"

Jenny's jaw almost dropped. Anything they should know? Like, how badly Jenny wanted to kiss Easy? To run her hands through his hair? That she was—*eek!*—going to go riding with him on Sunday? "Uh, no . . . I mean, Easy's cool. I like him." And before she could stop herself, the words kept tumbling out of her mouth. "I mean, as a friend. You know, we're in art class together. But that's it."

Tinsley nodded but didn't say anything. Callie continued to brush her hair and watch Jenny in the mirror. Jenny couldn't bear to look at Brett, who knew about her crush on Easy but wasn't saying anything.

Jenny felt herself start to panic, and she wasn't exactly thinking straight. This moment, with the four of them hanging out in their dorm room, getting ready for bed, was the sort of scenario she had dreamed about—she *had* to be in their secret society. This was her chance to be one of them. How could she let it slip through her fingers?

"Come on," Jenny said reasonably. "Easy could never be interested in me like that, anyway. Not after *you*, Callie." Jenny almost choked on the words, they were so hard to say. But she wasn't making it up—she sort of believed it as she was saying it. "You're like a movie star. I'm just . . . me."

Callie's nose twitched as she looked at her own reflection. Jenny could picture her thinking it over, maybe even imagining how silly Easy would look with *her*, short-little-I'm-just-me Jenny Humphrey. Jenny bit her lip.

Callie spun around abruptly and gave Tinsley a sly grin. "She's right. Easy is a little tall for her." The two of them shared the same satisfied look on their faces, and Jenny suddenly felt a hundred times worse than she had before she'd opened her big fat mouth.

"Good." Tinsley clapped. "That's settled, then. Welcome to Café Society, Jenny. I know we're going to end up great friends."

Jenny bit her lip even harder. Somehow she wasn't so sure.

To: CallieVernon@waverly.edu,
BrettMesserschmidt@waverly.edu;
SageFrancis@waverly.edu;
CelineColista@waverly.edu;
BennyCunningham@waverly.edu;
AlisonQuentin@waverly.edu;
JennyHumphrey@waverly.edu;
VerenaArneval@waverly.edu

From: TinsleyCarmichael@waverly.edu

Date: Friday, September 13, 10:05 a.m.

Subject: Café Society

My dearest, loveliest, ever-sumptuous friends,

You are all officially invited on a new adventure called Café Society, a secret club for only the most interesting and charming Waverly Owls. We are young and sexy creatures. Our society mantra is: Dress it. Act it. Be it. Flaunt it.

First unofficial meeting takes place tomorrow. 7 p.m. sharp. Ritoli's.

Please note: Proper attire required. Boyfriends are grounds for immediate expulsion. Bring your favorite libations (incognito) and your sense of mischief.

Yours in love and misbehavior,

T

To: RufusHumphrey@poetsonline.com
From: JennyHumphrey@waverly.edu
Date: Friday, September 13, 5:55 p.m.
Subject: THANK YOU!

Dear Dad,

I am running to dinner right now, but get this: I'm emailing you FROM MY NEW PHONE. How awesome is that??? Thank you sooooo much. I promise to write more over the weekend.

Love you,

Jenny

P.S. Tell Vanessa I say thank you too!

P.P.S. I always liked those rainbow suspenders. No, seriously!

OwlNet   Instant Message Inbox

Eric Dalton: Got your email. Interesting field trip idea.

TinsleyCarmichael: I thought you might be into it.

Eric Dalton: Yes, very . . .

14

WITH PROPER GROOMING, EVEN COMIC BOOK GEEKS CAN BE SEXY OWLS.

Tinsley stepped into the Waverly dining hall ten minutes before the Friday night dinner hour officially ended, fully aware that people had been waiting for her to appear. The dining hall was an exquisite building with cavernous cathedral ceilings and brightly colored stained glass windows, enormous oak tables, and heavy padded oak chairs that many of the smaller, waiflike girls had difficulty pulling out. The entrance was at the exact opposite side of the hall as the food service area, so once you entered, you still had to cross the room in front of hundreds of watching eyes to pick up your tray and start piling on chicken cordon bleu or whatever dreck was being served that evening. Tinsley didn't give it a second thought, whereas most people who walked into the dining hall alone were acutely aware of the long, tortuous journey they had to make before they could hide themselves behind the enormous plastic cereal containers.

She took in the scene, her eyes scanning the tables expertly for the faces of her friends. She spotted Benny and Brett and the boys at one of their usual long tables near the fireplace. She gave them a nod, being careful not to look at Brett, and continued toward the food line.

She picked up one of the beige plastic trays and noticed Heath Ferro waiting to be dished a plate of steaming eggplant parmesan. The sight of his tight butt in his brown Lacoste vintage track pants with the gold stripes down the side made Tinsley smile. She stepped up close behind him and said in a throaty voice, directly into his ear, before he could turn around, "Guess who—otherwise you get a shortie."

Heath chuckled as he reached for the plate from the dining hall worker and set it down on his tray. "You're not going to fool me with that voice, Tinsley. I hear it in my dreams. If you want to pull down my pants, you just have to ask."

Tinsley groaned, and Heath turned around, his gold-flecked green eyes blinking lazily as he focused on her apple-red lips. Tinsley bumped her hip against his, then slid her tray down the metal rails toward the green beans.

Lon Baruzza stood behind the glass counter in front of the giant tub of beans, holding an enormous spoon and wearing a white apron and a Notre Dame cap. He was a scholarship kid from Chicago, and Tinsley was always pleased to see him, even if the poor guy had to schlep beans onto plates for spoiled-rotten rich kids—he was much cuter than any of the other dining hall workers.

"I see you're in charge of the beans today," Tinsley said. "Is that a promotion from yesterday's creamed corn?"

"Nah," said Lon, who, even though he was dating Tricia Rieken, clearly liked handing a plate of food to Tinsley. "It's actually a demotion—they caught me smoking on my break yesterday. So only green vegetables for me from now on."

"That's good," said Tinsley. "I only took the corn yesterday because I wanted to say hi. I prefer beans." As he handed her a plate over the counter, she flashed him her ultra-flirtatious smile and glanced around for Heath, who had moved on to the hamburger station, obviously sulking that she was talking to Lon. She smiled to herself. One of her great pleasures in life was flirting with boys in front of other boys. It made them realize they had no claims on her.

She slid her tray next to Heath's as he struggled with an unwieldy pair of tongs to try and pick up a sesame bun and pretended not to notice her approach. Eventually he gave up and grabbed it with his hand.

"Gross," said Tinsley. "Those are there for a reason, so guys like you don't get their grubby paws all over other people's food." She expertly maneuvered the tongs and dropped a bun on her plate.

"Oh, didn't notice you were there. Thought you were still flirting with Baruzza," Heath said in mock surprise. She could tell he wasn't really bothered by it—Heath was her male coun-terpart, always knowing when to flash his devastating grin and when to give a playful wink. If anyone understood the thrill behind harmless flirtations, he did.

"I'm sorry, sweetheart. I'll never talk to another boy again. Happy?" Tinsley stabbed an overcooked garden burger with the extra-long fork and let it drop onto her plate. Ever since her father had produced a documentary about slaughterhouses when she was eight, Tinsley couldn't eat any sort of red meat. It gave her the creeps. Unfortunately, the decision not to buy leather didn't come so easily.

"You're just pissed at me because we won't let you join our secret society." Heath winked at her over his shoulder as he headed to the fountain soda machine, plucked a glass from the towering stack, and filled it halfway with Pepsi, then filled it the rest of the way with Dr Pepper. Tinsley followed him and filled her glass with Diet Pepsi.

"Not exactly. I just went ahead and started my own. Girls only."

"What are you going to do—have tickle fests? In your underwear?" Heath licked his lips at the thought.

"A little more sophisticated than that. And a little racier."

"Oh, yeah?" Heath said, liking the sound of that. "Maybe our secret societies should have a secret meeting together. Someplace sexy and off-limits." Heath sounded like he had been joking when he started the thought, but then a dreamy look came across his face, as if suddenly he was visualizing a clandestine meeting where Tinsley and Jenny and the other girls, in their bras and panties, smacked each other with expensive feather pillows, their hair getting all tousled and staticky. "Like Boston. We'll rent out a couple of suites at the Ritz-Bradley."

Tinsley set her glass down on her tray. She had a vision of two enormous, stylish suites at the Ritz, the door connecting them wide open as girls in flapper dresses and boys in tuxes flitted back and forth, passing around flutes of champagne and sharing elegant, chic embraces. "That might just be the best idea you've ever had, Ferro."

Heath continued. "We could all wear costumes, à la *Super Friends*."

"Whoa, now you're getting away from me."

"Seriously. Didn't you see that *OC* episode where Summer dressed up as Wonder Woman? That was like the sexiest thing ever." Heath set down his tray and stared at Tinsley objectively. "You would make a great Wonder Woman. You've got the body. And the hair." Heath took the opportunity to reach out and touch Tinsley's long black locks. She batted his hand away, although she could definitely imagine herself as a comic book hero, with black waves of hair highlighted with blue. And wearing a hot little outfit, of course. "And the Ritz will be like our League of Justice."

She stared at him blankly. "Our League of Justice?"

"You know, our headquarters. Our home base. For our missions?"

"Now you're starting to scare me. Can we get serious for a moment? We need to make this happen." Tinsley grabbed some silverware from the plastic tubs and glanced up toward their table of friends, who were finishing their meal by now. Callie waved.

"I'm totally with you." Heath agreed. "Next weekend, at the Ritz. We can book suites right next to each other."

"We'll dress up. Not as superheroes," she added quickly, notic-ing Heath's excitement. "Just dressy." She thought slyly of the outfit she was planning on wearing on her New York City date with Dalton—the sexy, coral chiffon flapper dress, its snug-fitting torso and flouncy skirt covered with delicate silver beading.

"Trust me. There's nothing sexier than Wonder Woman's leotard."

"That may be. But we're going for something a little more sophisticated."

Heath shook his head. "Not possible."

"I have to say, I've never seen this side of you before, Heath."

"What side?"

"This geek side."

Heath pretended to growl at her. "Do not start ragging on comic books. Please. I think highly of you and don't want that to change."

Tinsley smiled. She liked that Heath wasn't afraid she'd think he was a dork. And it was endearing that he got so excited at the thought of Wonder Woman in her leotard. Maybe one day she'd have to get that outfit just to give him a heart attack. She looked around and noticed that Benny, Callie, Alan, and Teague were all watching the two of them, wondering why they weren't coming over to the table. "Let's go sit down. We'll talk about this later, Batman."

"You're laughing now," he warned. "Go ahead, I'm going to snag a cookie."

Tinsley headed to the table by herself, noticing Callie staring sadly across the dining hall.

She followed Callie's line of sight and saw what she was looking at: Easy. He was sitting at a table with Jenny and Alison
Quentin and some of the other arty kids. They were all laughing
uproariously.

"You okay, Cal?" Tinsley asked as she set her tray down.
"Jenny promised there was nothing going on with them."

"I know." A full tray of food sat in front of Callie, untouched.
"But I'm not so sure. Are you?"

"Of course there's nothing going on," Tinsley replied. How
could there be? Jenny was short and practically disfigured, her
breasts were so gigantic. Tinsley glanced back at the art-geek
table. Easy was listening rapturously to Jenny, grinning and
blinking his dark eyelashes contentedly. *Uh-oh.* She *knew* that
look. It was the look of total, complete adoration he'd given her
the night they'd hooked up in Alaska, the same look she'd somewhat jealously watched him give Callie a hundred times. There
certainly *was* something going on there. Or would be soon. She
was sure of it.

"I just . . ." Callie interrupted her epiphany. She picked up
her fork and then put it down again. "I just wish I didn't have
to see him every day, you know? Like every time I think I feel
okay, I see him walking across the quad or sitting at dinner
laughing with Jenny." She motioned to the table across the
room.

Tinsley suddenly remembered seeing Easy and Jenny coming
out of the woods together on Wednesday afternoon, looking all
conspiratorial. That bastard. What was he *doing*, breaking
Callie's heart for that twerp? How *dare* he?

Tinsley narrowed her eyes, watching the way Easy gazed at Jenny. Even from across the large room, Tinsley could tell that the two of them were in their own world. Not for long, though, if she had anything to say about it. "You probably wish he'd, like, disappear or something, huh?" Tinsley suggested.

"Yeah." Callie stabbed a piece of broccoli and examined it.

Well, Tinsley thought. *Maybe I can make that happen.*

OwlNet

BrettMesserschmidt: So it looks like you can stop avoiding the room now, J.

Jenny Humphrey: I'm psyched.

BrettMesserschmidt: So you and EZ aren't . . .

Jenny Humphrey: No . . . nothing's happened, but, you know.

BrettMesserschmidt: Yup.

Jenny Humphrey: U were quiet last night.

BrettMesserschmidt: It's over. Officially.

Jenny Humphrey: I'm so sorry. U okay?

BrettMesserschmidt: Yeah . . . but would you mind asking me again later to be sure?

Jenny Humphrey: U can count on it.

15

A CAUTIOUS OWL

IS A WAVERLY OWL.

Brandon loved Saturday mornings at Waverly. Friday night parties were never as wild or liquor-fueled as Saturday night ones, and students didn't walk around looking as totally destroyed as they did on Sunday mornings. Saturday mornings always felt more wholesome, with girls and boys wearing their maroon Waverly sweatshirts tied around their waists, headed to the fields to watch the soccer matches or field hockey games. Kids from the city took the train down to spend the weekend in their Upper East Side penthouses, bar-hopping at night with their beautiful friends from private school or other New England prep schools. Brandon was from Connecticut—Greenwich born and raised—and while the gorgeously manicured grounds of Waverly were not exactly a landscape foreign to him, Waverly felt much more like home than Connecticut did. His father had remarried three years ago, and his stepmother was a total nightmare of a woman, barely ten years older than Brandon, and now his half-sibling two-year-old twins toddled around the house, gnawing and barfing on expensive furniture while their mother fawned over how brilliant they were. His stepmother, whose name he vowed would never cross his lips, seemed to be convinced he was gay and told him once that if he ever came out of the closet, his father would "probably still love him." At least he never got homesick.

The day was sunny but with a crispness to it. Brandon cut across the quad, his Bruno Magli slip-on loafers collecting bits of grass still damp with dew. He headed toward Maxwell Hall, an H. H. Richardson building that housed the student center, coffee bar, mail room, and study lounges and served as the social nexus of the campus. The library was the place to go when you were studying for a test or writing a paper that you couldn't afford to get a C on. People who went to Maxwell were interested in a more-social type of studying, the lazy kind that welcomes the noise of cappuccino machines and interruptions from attractive members of the opposite sex. Maybe Callie would be there, having her double shot of espresso and reading the latest copy of *Vanity Fair* instead of doing her calculus. Brandon was planning to flop down in an oversized armchair in one of the balcony alcoves for a few hours, sip his latte, and get started on de Tocqueville's *Democracy in America,* a book so boring that if the Founding Fathers had been required to read it, they would have certainly established a dictatorship instead.

The main space of Maxwell, with its massive stone walls, Romanesque arches, and enormous fireplace that was never actually lit, felt cavelike and welcoming. It was crowded with people, and after Brandon added his three packets of Splenda to his drink, he headed up the creaky back stairs to one of the dark alcoves on the upper floor, where you could look down onto the main lounge area and see everyone who came in.

At first Brandon was disappointed to see a thatch of dark curls instead of Callie's long blond locks, but then he recognized them as belonging to Jenny. "Hey," he said, pleased that she had somehow found her way to his favorite spot in the entire building. There were two oversized armchairs angled toward each other, a small wooden table between them. Brandon had spent many hours seated here with his iPod, longing for Callie. There was something so intimate about reading next to someone, every now and then looking up to catch their eye and maybe kiss a little.

Jenny glanced up from her book, clearly deep in thought. It took her a moment to focus on Brandon, but when she did, her face broke into a sweet grin. Her cheeks were a rosy pink, and her small, slightly upturned nose was dotted with freckles. She was wearing a flowered button-down from J.Crew that wasn't exactly tight yet still managed to hug her curves, a short distressed jean skirt, black tights, and gray suede flats so small they looked like kids' shoes. Her legs were crossed daintily at the ankles. "Hey, Brandon! What's up?"

Brandon was momentarily distracted by the movement of Jenny's breasts when she sat up straighter, but he didn't want to be one of those guys who could only stare at a girl's chest, no matter how inviting it might look, so he forced his eyes to return to her face. "Do you mind if I sit here?" he asked, indicating the other armchair.

"Of course not. It was getting kind of lonely up here with just me and Emma Bovary."

Brandon laughed in response, realizing he hadn't thought about Callie for at least thirty seconds. See, he wasn't obsessed. He remembered how he didn't want to speak to anyone for weeks after Callie had dumped him. Hopefully it wouldn't take her that long to get over Easy. Brandon slumped into the chair next to Jenny, setting his cup on the table between them. "How is Callie doing?" He lowered his voice, then suddenly felt absurd speaking so gravely about a breakup. It wasn't like Callie was in a coma or anything.

Jenny shrugged her petite shoulders. "I haven't seen too much of her. Tinsley and Brett have been spending time with her, mostly." Jenny paused and bit her lip. "I don't think she'd really pick me to talk to about it anyway," she added, her brown eyes dropping guiltily.

"Does that mean there really is something going on with you and Walsh?" Brandon demanded. He was glad to have Easy out of Callie's life, but he didn't exactly want him in Jenny's either. And it made him feel bad for Callie since he knew too well how much it sucked to see the person you loved in the arms of someone else immediately after you broke up.

Jenny met his eyes again. "I really don't know," she admitted. "I mean, we're friends, but—"

Brandon sat back in his chair. "Well, I hope it works out," he interrupted. The words came out colder than he had intended.

He wished Jenny well with Easy; he really did. But he didn't want Callie to end up hating Jenny as much as he hated Easy. Especially since they had to *live* together.

"I don't know what it is about him," Jenny gushed breathlessly.

I do, Brandon thought. *He's tall and looks like a Ralph Lauren model. He rides horses and he's artsy and "deep."* He tried not to roll his eyes. *What's not to love?*

"Just, you know, try to remember how much it's going to suck for Callie for a while. I mean, it's a small campus. It'll be hard for her to get away from it."

Brandon was suddenly reminded of how he had walked into the mail room the very day after Callie broke up with him to see her and Easy leaning against a wall of mailboxes, making out, Callie wearing the aqua Diane von Furstenberg cashmere wrap sweater that Brandon had given her for their one-year anniversary. She hadn't done it to be cruel, he knew—Callie never intentionally caused people pain. Well, not him, anyway. But just the thought that she was so swept away by Easy she didn't even think twice about where that sweater had come from, and what it meant, made Brandon want to go over there and punch Easy in his perfectly crooked smile.

"It's a small *dorm room*," Jenny pointed out. "And I feel really weird already. Not that there's anything going on between us yet. It just might be *headed* that way."

Brandon nodded. "What do you think my chances are of getting Callie back?" he asked, a little sheepish. He was so gorgeous, Jenny thought. He could have his pick of most

Waverly girls, but still, it was only Callie he wanted. It occurred to her that if Callie understood how easy it was to get swept away by Easy Walsh and completely forget about a guy as great as Brandon, she might forgive Jenny for getting swept away by Easy too. She sighed. Or maybe not.

"I think right now she probably just wants some space." Jenny took a sip of her now-cold green tea. "She doesn't want to go out with anyone yet. Besides, we're kind of in this new society, and no boyfriends allowed."

Brandon groaned. "You're in Tinsley's secret society too?" He unzipped his leather messenger bag, so exquisitely aged it looked like it was from World War II, and pulled out a small book. He needed to at least pretend to be getting some work done.

"Yeah," Jenny admitted, still excited that she had gotten the email from Tinsley yesterday. Maybe Tinsley was willing to forgive her for being the awkward new girl who stole her bed after all. Tinsley was the crown queen of Waverly. Hands down the coolest, most beautiful girl on campus, the kind of person who didn't wait around for cool stuff to happen—she went out and *made* it happen. If Jenny couldn't *be* Tinsley, being friends with her was the next-best thing. Maybe some of the glamour would rub off on her. "It sounds like fun."

"Of course it does," Brandon said with a smile. "Tinsley doesn't involve herself in things that aren't fun."

"That doesn't sound like a bad way to be, necessarily."

Brandon hesitated. "It's more than a way of life for Tinsley. She's turned amusing herself into an art form. No matter the cost."

Jenny leaned back in her chair and tried to digest Brandon's words. She could see that he had a point—after all, Tinsley had been suspended from Waverly for having "fun"—yet it didn't seem to take away from any of Tinsley's allure. If anything, it added to it. Tinsley did what she wanted. "Hey, if it means she's going to be nice to me, I'll take it. Between her and Callie, I spent all week afraid to go to my room."

"Just be careful," Brandon advised, his golden brown eyes suddenly serious. Usually Jenny thought it was unfair when such gorgeous lashes were wasted on a boy, but they made Brandon look so elegant. He reminded her of a silent movie star with his smooth jaw, expressive eyes, and strategically disheveled hair. And he was *nice.* Callie didn't know how lucky she was to have a guy like him crazy about her.

"I came from a school that was filled with girls like Tinsley." Jenny would never forget the Blair Waldorfs she had grown up half fearing, half longing to be, girls who made you feel like you didn't exist until they happened to need something from you. They'd assume you'd be willing to drop everything for them, which, of course, you would. But the truly dangerous girls were the Serena van der Woodsens of the world because they were so perfectly beautiful and *nice,* they were almost inhuman. Tinsley was somewhere in between—she had all the apparent perfections of a Serena, yet her mind was always scheming like a Blair, always wanting more. "I can handle her." But Jenny was suddenly completely unsure of herself. She'd never be a Blair or a Serena or a Tinsley, only a Jenny. Would she always be a wannabe?

"Well, there's something freaky about Tinsley—she makes you want to be her friend, but you can't trust her. *Ever.*"

He was so fervent, Jenny wondered if something had happened between them. "All right. I'll sleep with one eye open."

Brandon chuckled. "That's not a bad idea."

16

A WAVERLY OWL NEVER ABANDONS HER COMMITMENTS.

UNLESS SHE HAS A REALLY, REALLY GOOD REASON.

Dear Mr. Dalton, I'm afraid I will no longer be able to assist you with your office tasks. I will, of course, continue my work on the Disciplinary Committee as class prefect, as I am serious about my commitment to that position. Thank you for understanding. Brett looked at the note, written in her backwards-slanting cursive on one of her lime green Crane's monogrammed correspondence cards. Was it too personal to use one of them? Maybe she should just email him. But no, it felt like a more suitable ending to their ill-fated affair to write the note on her expensive stationery, with the BLM engraved in the corner. Maybe, she thought wistfully, it would make him wonder what her middle name was. Also, it made her feel like a heroine from a Jane Austen novel, a wounded female so elegant that she managed to write such a polite letter to the man who had scorned her.

Not that she was angry. She just felt deflated and confused. If Eric hadn't wanted anything to happen between them, he'd had plenty of opportunities to stop things. But he'd encouraged her, hadn't he? Brett hated that she felt so defensive about it, wondering if she had only imagined there was ever anything between them.

No, that wasn't right, Brett answered herself as she crossed campus to Stansfield Hall, unlocked but generally silent on weekends. She thought back to the first time she'd met Eric Dalton, thinking at first that he was a student. She was unable to shake the feeling that from the very beginning, while he'd been kind of sheepish about his attraction to her, he still never tried to hide it. And it wasn't just a casual flirtation—he invited her out to dinner, took her in his plane to his home in Newport, and had drinks waiting for her on his sailboat. He'd given her wine, lit candles for her, sent cars to pick her up and take her back to campus, invited her to spend the night with him, taken her clothes off. . . . These were not actions of a man afraid of being inappropriate.

She climbed the three flights of marble stairs to his office, her heels echoing loudly, and then paused when she heard a shuffling noise inside and music playing softly. Silently she placed her note directly in front of the door and tiptoed back down the long hallway.

An hour later the sun was getting lower in the afternoon sky and Brett was still aimlessly wandering around campus. It was a glorious Indian summer afternoon, and she was too depressed to go indoors and spend her Saturday in the library alone, without even a cute boy to IM.

Brett wiped her nose pathetically on the back of her hand. She hadn't spoken to Jeremiah for a week now, not since Black Saturday, when he caught her coming off Dalton's sailboat at the docks. Suddenly she felt a tug of longing in her stomach, remembering how nice it had been to just hang out with Jeremiah and smoke Parliaments and rag on their families together. She found herself missing his Boston accent that just last week she'd found so annoying.

Without thinking about what she was doing, Brett's Jimmy Choo slides led her along the path past the northern end of Waverly's campus toward the old cemetery. Callie thought she was morbid to like hanging out there, but it was a secluded space, the most modern gravestone dating from the late 1800s, and she and Jeremiah had always found it peaceful and romantic beneath the canopy of forest, set back from the main road. It was a long walk, past the Waverly gatehouse. She remembered how excited she'd been the night Dalton's car had come to pick her up. She shook her head, trying to forget how stupid and childish she'd been, and concentrated instead on the gorgeous, sunny afternoon.

But when she stepped through the massive rusted iron gate, she noticed a familiar athletic body leaning against the moss-covered stone wall. Her breath caught in her throat. Jeremiah. Whoa. Had she conjured him up somehow?

Jeremiah glanced up at the sound of someone approaching and did a double take when he saw Brett. She froze for a second, not sure if she should approach him, but then a welcoming smile broke across his lips. *"Hey,"* he said, happily looking her up and down.

Brett flipped her Oliver Peoples gold-mirrored sunglasses on top of her head and tried not to blush. She stopped awkwardly several feet from Jeremiah, not sure if she should give him a hug or what. *"Hey,"* she replied. "I thought you'd have a game today."

"Nah, it was last night. We killed 'em. Coach took me out in the fourth." Jeremiah blushed modestly and hoisted himself onto the stone wall behind him. "It's good to see you again."

"You too," she admitted shyly.

"How've you been?" His wide-set blue eyes were bright and happy-looking.

Brett found herself slightly distracted by Jeremiah's familiar fresh-from-the-showers smell. She kicked at a tuft of grass and then heaved herself up on the stone wall next to him, her shoes dangling several feet above the ground. "Been better." She shrugged and peeked at him through a curtain of her red hair, noticing his concerned frown. "You don't want to hear about it."

"How do you know if you don't give me the chance?" He leaned back on his elbows, his floppy auburn hair falling away from his face. "I'm a good listener." Jeremiah *was* a fantastic listener, patient and always interested in whatever she had to say. It would be totally bizarre to talk to him about the whole Eric Dalton situation, and totally selfish. But Jeremiah was the kindest, most straightforward person she'd ever met—if he didn't want to know, he wouldn't be asking.

Brett took a deep breath and stared at one of the crumbling gravestones in front of them. "I just . . . well, I haven't been myself at all lately, you know?" She peeked through her lashes at him. "I was sort of swept away by something. I, uh, I don't know how much you know. . . ." Brett trailed off, feeling guilty and disgusted with herself.

"Well, I think I know the basics." He flashed her an encouraging smile. "Word travels fast. The story is, you got swept off your feet by the notorious, charming Mr. Dalton." Jeremiah cleared his throat. "More than that—you'd have to tell me."

"Well, I guess that's an adequate synopsis." Brett laughed dryly. "It's pretty stupid, really. . . . We just, sort of, started spending a lot of time together, and I guess I was just kind of convinced that he, you know, *liked* me." Brett sighed and pulled her feet up on top of the stone wall. "Until I got an IM from him the other day that sort of said, 'It's been nice, but it's over.'" She shrugged again. "And that was it."

Jeremiah exhaled a long breath, as if he had been holding it the whole time Brett was talking. "Well, do you want to hear my professional opinion?"

Brett giggled. She was surprised how good it felt to share what had happened with someone. Or maybe it was just Jeremiah? "Yes, please."

"The way I see it, you didn't imagine *anything*. Obviously Dalton liked you—why wouldn't he? You're Ms. Brett Lenore Messerschmidt—the smartest, hottest, most talented redhead to come through Waverly since Rita Hayworth. Of course he couldn't resist." Jeremiah smiled, and though his tone was friendly, Brett thought she detected a note of bitterness. "Until suddenly—maybe he realized he was breaking the law *and* violating every single teacherly ethic imaginable—he remembered that, wait a second, you're sixteen. He's an *adult*. He should have known better."

Suddenly Brett was reminded of the time Jeremiah had taken her to Fenway Park to see the Red Sox play. His parents had season tickets for seats that were practically on top of the field. They were so close Brett thought she could smell the players' sweat—gross, but also kind of sexy. She was busy staring at the super-hot center fielder when a foul ball was sent careening toward her head—she didn't even notice it until Jeremiah reached in front of her and caught it with his bare hand the second before it smacked her in the face. Everyone around them started congratulating Jeremiah on his nice catch, but he ignored them—he just wanted to make sure Brett was okay.

And now, after everything, he was still every bit as sweet.

"Rita Hayworth went to Waverly?"

"No," Jeremiah said. "But that's the only part that isn't true."

Brett felt a goofy grin spread across her face, and she pretended to pry a pebble out of her shoe. She couldn't believe how much better she felt after talking to Jeremiah for only ten minutes.

"So, did you, uh, you know . . ." Jeremiah started in a low voice, trailing off at the end.

"Have sex with him? No!" Brett definitely detected relief on his face when she said that. God, what if she had? Instead of regretting *not* sleeping with Eric, Brett suddenly felt relief wash over her whole body. What a horrible mistake it would have been. Even in the warm afternoon, she shivered.

An hour later, they were lying on their backs on top of the stone wall, staring at the swatches of blue sky between the yellowing leaves and still talking. Brett abruptly sat up to check her watch. "I've gotta get back for the silly Café Society meeting," she said wistfully. "But thanks for listening to me blab about, you know, everything. It's been . . . nice. To talk to you again. Even about this." Brett blinked her catlike eyes at Jeremiah. She hoped he knew how sorry she was for hurting him, but she wasn't about to bring it up, not when they'd had such a nice afternoon.

"Hey, about your society? I was talking to Teague Williams at a scrimmage last week, and he mentioned a trip to Boston. . . ." Jeremiah kicked his heels against the stone wall. "I was thinking I'd go if that's okay with you."

She smiled. "I'd like that."

"Okay, good. Now . . . are you sure you don't want me to punch his lights out?" Jeremiah hopped off the wall and swung a right hook at the air. "Get a couple of the offensive linemen to go over to his house and scare him?" he joked.

"Thanks." Brett laughed. "But that's all right." She slid down off the wall, landing in front of Jeremiah and stumbling a little before he put out his hand to steady her. "Thanks," she whispered again, and before he could say anything, she wrapped her arms around him and buried her head in his chest, giving him a quick hug. His body stiffened in surprise, and he patted her back gently before pulling away.

"Don't ever feel bad when things don't work out between you and an asshole like that," he said softly. "It just means that you're too good for him."

"I think you might be missing your calling as a cheerleader," Brett said, realizing that the whole time they'd been hugging, she'd been holding her breath. "I'll see you soon, okay?"

Jeremiah smiled, but she couldn't read what he was thinking. "All right. Have fun tonight." He turned quickly and walked away, and as Brett made her way back to Dumbarton to get ready for the first secret society meeting, she rubbed her arms. She had goose bumps, and she was more confused now than she had been when she'd set out that afternoon. But somehow it was a much, much more pleasant confusion.

OwlNet   Instant Message Inbox

AlanStGirard: Want a beer before dinner? Crater?

HeathFerro: Word.

AlanStGirard: Buchanan coming?

HeathFerro: Nah, he's in one of his moods. You know, listening to Natalie Merchant all day and pouting.

AlanStGirard: He'd better be over it by the Boston trip. He wouldn't miss out on that, would he?

HeathFerro: U kidding? Leave Callie alone in the clutches of us animals? Not bloody likely!

17

A PROPER OWL DOES NOT ATTEMPT TO SNAG

THE PIZZA GUY.

Jenny walked up the Dumbarton steps, hoping to catch her roommates getting ready for the Café Society meeting. She loved the idea of the four of them getting dressed together. Maybe Tinsley would loan Jenny a top—well, maybe not a top because of the discrepancy in their bust sizes—or a belt or something, saying, "This would look great on you." Jenny had always wanted a sister. Sharing a room with three other girls was the next-best thing. But when she pushed open the door of Dumbarton 303 expectantly, she found it empty, with only a trace of Tinsley's Dior J'adore lingering in the air.

Jenny sighed and started to flip through her closet hesitantly, not wanting to over- or under-dress since Tinsley had made a point of mentioning "appropriate dress required" in her email. She pulled her dressiest trousers from their hanger, her royal blue silk and cotton-blend Philosophy di Alberta Ferretti ones that had cost her five months' allowance at the Barneys Warehouse Sale. They were the kind of pants that managed to look sexy and sophisticated and hide all of the wearer's flaws. No wonder rich people always looked so beautiful. They could afford to buy clothes this well made. Jenny tried pulling on a white satin Calvin Klein baby doll camisole that she'd bought without trying it on from the sale rack at Saks, but it somehow made her look pregnant *and* slutty at the same time. She crumpled it up and threw it in the corner. A few other tops piled up in the corner before she settled on a sequined lace-trim silk tank in silver and her navy, sleek-fitting Ben Sherman blazer.

"Someone looks fabulous!" Brett cried as she barreled through the door breathlessly and immediately undressed. Brett glanced at her closet for half a second before grabbing a pair of Stuart Weitzman peep-toe pumps in dark silver satin with a vintage jeweled brooch on top. Jenny had seen them in *InStyle* and was shocked when Brett handed them to her, saying, "You're a six, right? These would look great on you."

"How'd you know I was a six?"

Brett looked sheepish. "Well, I tried on those burgundy suede boots under your bed the other day. I'm a six and a half, and I *had* to see if they fit."

Jenny laughed, pulling Brett's shoes onto her delicate feet. "You can borrow them anytime. If they're not too uncomfortable." She turned around to find Brett fully dressed, made up, hair freshly brushed, boots on, dabbing one of her mini Chanel perfume bottle to her wrists.

"Wow, you're fast," Jenny remarked in total awe.

When they entered Ritoli's, the other girls were already there, sitting around one of the large circular tables in the corner. Callie, Benny, Verena, and Tinsley all wore dresses that looked like they'd come directly from the runway.

"Take your seats, my ladies," Tinsley greeted them grandly, taking a sip of some unidentifiable fizzy pink stuff from a Nalgene bottle on the table. "We're still waiting for Sage and—who else?"

"Celine," Callie answered promptly, clearly the second in command.

"There they are." Verena waved her ring-clad fingers at Sage and Celine, who had just stepped through the door. Brett sat down next to her, and Jenny sat down in the empty seat beside Alison Quentin, the pretty Korean girl in her art class.

"Hi, everyone." Jenny felt like the new girl again, but she was grateful to be included in a gathering of these pretty, popular girls. She pulled out one of the plastic sports bottles that she and Brett had filled with cheap merlot and set it down on the table.

"What have you got there?" Alison burped. "Benny and I have been drinking vodka lemonades since three." She nodded wistfully at her almost-empty Gatorade bottle.

"Really bad wine. You're welcome to it if you run out," Jenny offered as Celine Colista, in a burgundy Vera Wang strapless jersey dress and silver Manolo stilettos, strutted over to the table. Her black hair was freshly blown out.

"Damn," remarked Benny. "Daddy bought someone a new dress." Celine's father was an A-list director and had just made a film starring Kate Hudson and Mark Ruffalo, as Celine often reminded people.

"Nah," Celine said, twirling around a little to show off how perfectly the color complemented her olive skin. "He got it from wardrobe. Kate wears it in the film." She rested her hands on her tiny waist. "Of course, I had to have it taken in." Jenny met Brett's eyes, and they both stifled giggles.

"Are you guys all going to a party or something?" A gorgeous guy had come up to their table without anyone noticing, but now that he stood two feet away, all the girls were acutely aware of his presence. Jenny had seen him once before, when she stopped in for a slice one day after skipping lunch, but he looked even cuter than he had that day, wearing a simple black T-shirt and a pair of slightly baggy Abercrombie & Fitch drawstring khakis.

"This *is* the party, Angelo," Callie said coyly, her fingers tracing the edge of the leather menu. Jenny was a little surprised to hear how familiar Callie's tone was—did she know him?

"Well, I'm glad I'm working tonight, then." Angelo pulled a small pad of paper from the waistband of his pants.

"We are too," said Tinsley, winking. Clearly Angelo was psyched—it probably wasn't every night that a group of dressed-up half-drunk girls showed up, eager to flirt with him. Jenny took a gulp from her sports bottle, hoping it would help her feel a little less left out.

"You guys know what you want?"

"Mmm," said Sage Francis, tossing her platinum hair over her shoulder and leaning forward toward Angelo.

"How much pizza do you think we could eat?" Benny asked, definitely not willing to be left out. She batted her enormous dark brown eyes at Angelo.

Angelo looked them over, pretending to assess the situation with the eye of a pizza expert. Even Jenny felt herself shifting nervously, hoping he thought she was cute. "Well, you girls never eat as much as you should. You're all too skinny. I'd say you could use three larges." They all smiled. Who didn't enjoy being told they were thin? They debated for a minute, then decided on one with cheese and mushrooms, one with pesto sauce, and the third with pepperoni and olives.

"He is so fucking hot," Sage exclaimed as soon as Angelo walked away.

"Maybe I'll say something in Italian to him. . . ." Benny bit her lips, stained a light pink with Vincent Longo's Foolish Virgin lipstick. The color was a little dull, but Tinsley knew it was her favorite because of the name. Tinsley and Benny had once gotten drunk while studying for their European history final, and Benny had told her she considered herself a born-again virgin, without any of the religious implications, because she had accidentally lost it last Christmas break to a hot UPenn senior her parents had set her up with. She preferred not to count it, something that Tinsley found totally amusing.

Celine wrinkled her nose. "Isn't that kind of racist? Just because he's Italian doesn't mean he speaks it. I mean, just because Alison's Korean doesn't mean she speaks Korean, right?"

"I speak Korean," Alison admitted apologetically.

"I bet I could hook up with him before any of you guys could," Callie announced abruptly. Jenny stared at her, wondering where this sudden burst of recklessness was coming from. Callie looked wilder than normal tonight, trading her usually classic preppy look for an outfit she could have worn club-hopping with Lindsay Lohan: a flirty deep purple BCBG Max Azria halter dress with a tiered, pleated miniskirt. The dress had a plunging neckline that would look sleazy on anyone with breasts like Jenny's, but instead it just revealed Callie's bony breastplate. God, she needed to eat something, Jenny thought, wishing she could hand over some of her own extra weight—namely, from her DD breasts—to Callie.

"Fifty bucks says I can beat you to it," Benny countered cheerfully. Sage and Celine quickly jumped in.

"Angelo's hot." Tinsley leaned back in her chair, knowing that she looked gorgeous in her ecru Elie Tahari corset-inspired chiffon blouse. It set off her tan skin and dark hair, which framed her face in long, full waves. "But I prefer a more-mature guy."

"Maybe you can hook up with his father," Brett suggested, taking a long drink from her plastic bottle. They exchanged a charged glance, and Jenny wondered what was going on. She shivered a little, thinking of all the undercurrents she must be missing—these girls had known each other for years, and she had only just stepped in.

"That's a little *too* old." Tinsley smirked. "I couldn't date someone beyond his mid-twenties, no matter how well endowed he was."

"The whole family has a reputation for being hung like horses," Alison whispered to Jenny, who almost spat out the warm wine in her mouth.

"I'm sure someone could find out, right?" Jenny giggled boldly. She needed to get some food into her body fast, or she was going to be in trouble. Her head was already beginning to swim.

"I've gotta pee," Callie said ineloquently. She stood up and headed to the bathroom at the back of the restaurant, wobbling slightly on her heels.

Tinsley turned her blue-violet eyes to Jenny for the first time that night. "You could try finding out for yourself. Or do you have your eye on someone else?" Her tone was friendly and light, and if it had been anyone else but Tinsley asking, Jenny would have assumed she was just curious. But Tinsley had seen Jenny and Easy coming out of the woods, Jenny was sure of it now, and it seemed a little too convenient that she waited until Callie had left to bring it up, as if she hoped to goad Jenny into revealing something.

"That wouldn't be allowed, right?" Jenny asked innocently. "I thought boyfriends were banned."

"Excellent," Tinsley praised her with a wry smile. "You're paying attention." Their gaze locked across the table before Jenny pulled hers away and took another sip of her wine.

"Just boyfriends are banned, right?" said Celine nervously. "Not, like, hooking up with guys?"

"That, my dear, is encouraged," Tinsley announced regally, leaning back in her chair again. She looked like a panther, lean and strong and slightly bored, as if waiting for the perfect moment to pounce.

Angelo appeared with an enormous tray bearing three steaming pizzas. He expertly dished them out onto the girls' plates while they smiled flirtatiously at him. As Jenny held out her plate for Angelo, she caught him staring at her cleavage.

When she looked up to see if anyone else had noticed, she met Tinsley's knowing gaze. Suddenly all her hunger drained away. For whatever reason, Tinsley had her eye on her. And it was not a comfortable feeling.

RyanReynolds: How'd your first meeting go? Any naked table dancing?

BennyCunningham: The night is young. . . . We just left Ritoli's.

RyanReynolds: R u loaded?

BennyCunningham: Let's just say, the entire world is spinning right now and I've got the urge to go skinny dipping.

RyanReynolds: Save that for Boston. I hear the Ritz has Jacuzzis in every room.

OwlNet

TinsleyCarmichael: I've been drinking wine and thinking about you. . . .

EricDalton: Where are you?

TinsleyCarmichael: None of your beeswax.

EricDalton: Then when can I see you again?

TinsleyCarmichael: Soon enough. I hear that absence makes the heart grow fonder.

EricDalton: Or absence makes the heart grow tortured . . . Let's go to New York.

TinsleyCarmichael: Thought you'd never ask. I've always wanted to stay at 40 Banfield in Soho.

EricDalton: That can be arranged. Tuesday? We can both call in sick.

TinsleyCarmichael: A Waverly Owl Does Not Skip Class! Kidding. I like that idea.

EricDalton: Good.

TinsleyCarmichael: Speaking of cutting . . . I saw Easy Walsh skipping. . . . I know he's on probation.

EricDalton: Sounds like I'll have to have a word with him. That kid is trouble.

TinsleyCarmichael: You're telling me.

EricDalton: So Tuesday then? I'm looking forward to it.

TinsleyCarmichael: Of course you are.

18

A WAVERLY OWL NEVER USES AN EX-BOYFRIEND
AS A WEAPON.

The girls walked in a tight pack in the cool evening, bumping into each other as their delicate heels picked their way down the cobbled sidewalks of Rhinecliff. Callie was about to slow down a bit and wait for Tinsley to come up beside her and sling her arm through hers, but just then her tiny satin Jimmy Choo clutch began to vibrate. She thought for a brief, wonderful second that maybe it was Easy calling, but then she recognized the number as Brandon's. He was probably calling to check on her, make sure she wasn't too drunk, and while she didn't exactly want to hear it, she *was* drunk enough to crave a boy's voice.

"What's up, Brandon?" Her tongue felt slightly heavy in her mouth.

"Nothing." Brandon had a surprisingly deep phone voice, making him sound much older and more mysterious than he really was. "Just thought you might want to get coffee or something."

"We're on our way back from dinner. I don't know if I'm in the mood for coffee." Callie glanced over at Tinsley and noticed that she was instant messaging someone. Turning her head slightly, she could see that Benny and Alison were too. What the fuck? Everyone else's lives suddenly seemed so much more interesting and love-filled than hers. In a wave of self-pity, she wondered if hanging out with Brandon might boost her completely smashed ego. "Well, maybe."

"I'm just leaving Berk." Berkman-Meier was the music center, an enormous complex of concrete slab buildings, seventies style, that housed a large lecture hall where Waverly's various music groups performed, music classrooms, and dozens of small soundproof rooms for individual practice. Brandon's mother had been first violinist for the New York Philharmonic, and he played to be close to her. She'd died when he was only four, and it was the first thing she'd taught him to do, even before reading. It was sexy that Brandon was so good at something without even really trying—but Callie wished he were, like, a prodigy at the bass or an instrument with a little more rock-star cachet. "Want me to meet you at the front gate?"

Brandon was waiting for her at the gate when the pack of girls approached. Tinsley noticed him first and shot Callie a pointed look. "Looks like your *boyfriend* is waiting for you."

"I can't help it if I have admirers." Callie noticed Jenny looking away uncomfortably. It pissed her off to have a younger girl pitying her, especially one who had become so friendly with

Easy. At least Jenny had assured them that nothing was going on there. Callie was humiliated enough at being dumped, but being dumped because of *someone else* was ten times worse.

Brett winked at Callie over her shoulder as the rest of them continued on toward campus, shooting Brandon knowing looks and giggling as they passed.

"What was that all about?" Brandon demanded. He was wearing a neatly ironed pair of Paper Denim & Cloth jeans and a Brooklyn sweatshirt, even though he was from Greenwich. Callie was grateful he wasn't carrying his violin.

"They're just being stupid," Callie replied a little crankily, feeling her buzz drain away. Then she noticed him staring at her. No matter how irritated she could get with Brandon, she had to admit it felt nice to have someone look at her like that, as if he couldn't tear his eyes away.

"I just wanted to see how you were doing," he faltered, with a tender smile.

"Don't give me that fake sympathy. I know you're thrilled Easy dumped me." Callie pulled her almost-empty pack of Parliaments—she'd been smoking like a fiend lately—from the pocket of her True Religion jean jacket that used to fit her perfectly but now felt loose and annoying.

Brandon looked hurt. "I'm not sorry you're not with him anymore—he doesn't deserve to be with you. But I'm sorry you're feeling bad."

Callie sighed and lit her cigarette. Brandon was just so *nice*. Maybe that was the problem. Even after she broke up with him, he was sweet to her, letting her know he'd always be there for her and that he'd always love her. But while that seemed very noble of him, it didn't make him any more appealing. He just made it too *easy*. "I don't know. I'm probably getting what I deserve, right?"

"Callie, what you deserve is to be treated like the goddess you are." Brandon shook his head. "Don't let a slimebag like Easy bring you down." He took in her thin, drawn face and felt scared for a moment, realizing how skinny and sad she seemed. "You're just so far above him, it's crazy."

Callie sighed again. That was an easy thing to say to someone who'd just had their heart ripped out of their chest cavity and thrown onto the cold tile floor—he didn't deserve you, you're way too good for him, you can do so much better. Well, so what if Easy didn't deserve her—it didn't stop her from wanting *him*.

But then there was Brandon in his polo shirt with the Ralph Lauren horse emblem on the chest, his brown Calvin Klein wing tips shuffling nervously in the grass. At least she had the power to make one guy nervous in her presence.

"Easy could barely stand to look at me when he dumped me—it was like I was so repulsive, he wanted to erase every inch of me from his memory." Callie stared at the ground and ran her hands up and down her jacketed arms pitifully.

"That's so ridiculous! You are so fucking beautiful!" Brandon protested immediately, as she knew he would. Even if their whole interaction was totally predictable, Callie already felt better. After all, it wasn't like it was Tinsley or Brett trying to cheer her up—Brandon was a guy. Him thinking she was beautiful meant more. "I mean, God. It hurts me to even *look* at you sometimes."

"Why?"

Brandon shrugged. "Because I can't have you." He stared at her, willing her to contradict him, but Callie stayed silent for a moment, thinking about how badly she wished it were Easy standing here in the dark, cold evening, telling her these things.

But it wasn't Easy. It was Brandon, a guy Easy disliked, thinking him too sentimental and conservative and clearly repressed. A guy it would piss off Easy to know she was starting up with again—and around Waverly, word traveled fast.

Impulsively, Callie stepped toward Brandon and rested her thin hand on his bare arm. It shook a little when she touched it. "Are you just saying that to make me feel better?" she asked coyly.

"You know I mean it," he told her softly.

And so she leaned toward him and pressed her lips to his before he could say anything to change her mind. His mouth was soft and familiar and tasted like cinnamon gum, something new. When she felt him start to pull away, she pressed her body against his, hoping someone would walk by.

"Thank you," she tried to murmur sexily as she pulled away. "For being so sweet. You made my night." It was something a girl in a movie would have said.

Brandon touched her hair, stroking it gently like he used to. "You made my year." It made Callie sad suddenly because she had said her line without really meaning it the way Brandon had.

"Walk me back?" she asked, wanting to get out of there, wanting to check her email in case Easy had written, and wanting to curl up in her most favorite Natori silk pajamas when she found out he hadn't and cry herself to sleep.

OwlNet   Instant Message Inbox

EmilyJenkins:	Bitches didn't let me in their club, but I saw Callie sucking face with your roomie.
HeathFerro:	BRANDON??
EmilyJenkins:	The one and only.
HeathFerro:	U think it's to make EZ jealous?
EmilyJenkins:	Duh.

OwlNet   Instant Message Inbox

HeathFerro:	Yo, Callie's kissing Brandon outside.
EasyWalsh:	Um OK.
HeathFerro:	U don't care? EJ thinks it's to make you jealous. R u?
EasyWalsh:	Nah.
HeathFerro:	Dude, gimme sumthin!
EasyWalsh:	Fuck off, Ferro.

 **OwlNet**

To: Undisclosed Secret Society Recipients
From: HeathFerro@waverly.edu
Date: Sunday, September 15, 11:43 a.m.
Subject: Boston

Dear Superfriends,

That's right, you heard me. Time to look inside your soul and find your own superhero: maybe that's Wonder Woman, or maybe, if you're me, that's Hugh Hefner.

You have less than a week to prepare. Details to follow.

Fondling-ly yours,

HF

19

A WAVERLY OWL WEARS PROPER HEADGEAR WHEN
ENGAGED IN A DANGEROUS PHYSICAL ACTIVITY.

Jenny had Googled *horseback riding clothes*, so she felt
relatively prepared showing up at the stables on Sunday
afternoon for her riding date with Easy. The Web sites said
straight-leg jeans were the best if you didn't have jodhpurs,
which Jenny definitely didn't, so she wore a pair of straight-leg
Diesel jeans she'd had since seventh grade, when she'd stopped
growing. Well, growing taller—her chest had obviously continued to bloom. Her long hair fell into two braids down her back,
which she hoped gave her an air of boho chic and not an air of
insane-Heidi chick.

Even though it was clear that Callie was still reeling from
her breakup with Easy, Jenny couldn't stop thinking about
him. When Emma Bovary falls in love with Rodolphe, Jenny
gave him Easy's face, and when she later falls uncontrollably in
love with Léon, Jenny imagined he was as irresistible as Easy.

She just hoped she wouldn't bring disaster upon herself like poor silly Emma.

When she got to the stables, she saw Easy leading two horses out in the paddock, one black, one a deep chestnut. She watched for a minute, noticing how Easy's head was bent toward them as he patted them both on their necks, talking to them. His hands ran across the saddles and stirrups.

"Which one is Credo?" Jenny asked when Easy finally noticed her approaching.

He stroked the black one's sleek mane. "This is my sweetheart. Isn't she gorgeous?"

Jenny crept slowly toward Easy and his horse, not wanting to spook her. Credo was enormous. "Credo's a girl? She's so huge."

Easy laughed. "She's really not. I'm going to ride Dean Marymount's mare, Diana, because she's a lot bigger than Credo. And I told Credo to be gentle with you."

"Good," Jenny said, hesitantly touching the horse on her neck where Easy had been stroking her. Her coat was surprisingly soft and glossy. Credo shifted a little at Jenny's touch and turned her head to look at her. The quick movement startled Jenny, but she didn't flinch and instead kept petting the giant animal as she admired her enormous, brown-liquid eyes.

"Let her smell your hand," Easy said over her shoulder. "It will help her get to know you faster."

"Like this?" Jenny held her palm out awkwardly in front of Credo's nose. With anyone but Easy, she would have been terrified that the horse would bite her hand off, but she trusted him. Credo made a snuffling noise with her nostrils and nuzzled her soft, damp nose against Jenny's hand. Jenny giggled. "She looks so much happier than those poor horses in the city that have to pull carriages around Central Park for tourists all day."

"God, you're a city girl," Easy said affectionately. He held out a black velvet riding helmet. "Here," he said. "See if this fits."

"I have to wear a helmet? Does that mean there's a chance she's going to throw me off or something?" She held it awkwardly in her hands, suddenly scared again, visualizing her body flying through the air and landing in a crunch of bones against the hard, packed dirt.

"Nah, she likes you."

"How can you tell?"

Easy scratched his head. "Well, I can't tell for sure." He shrugged. "But she likes girls who are nice to me." He raised his eyebrows at her, causing her to forget all about being afraid of Credo. "So, you'd better be nice to me."

Right, she thought. *Like there was any danger of not being nice.*

Easy took the helmet from Jenny's hands and placed it on her head gently, then flattened his hand on top of it and rocked it back and forth and from side to side. Jenny could feel her scalp moving with it. "What are you doing?"

"Making sure it fits." He took his hand off her head and bent his knees so that his eyes were level with hers. He examined how the helmet fit around her head, his face just inches from hers, so she could practically count his eyelashes if she wanted to. His eyes finally met hers. "You look cute," he said softly.

"How come *you're* not wearing a helmet?"

"Because I'm not worried about me," he said sweetly, though

Jenny still thought it was unfair. She'd pictured her hair flying out behind her in the wind, but maybe next time. "Are you ready to get on?"

"Already?" she yelped, terrified.

"You want to stand here talking all day?"

Jenny looked up at him. "Sort of."

"Come on. It's fun, and you'll be fine. Credo knows what she's doing, and she's not going to break into a gallop or anything." Easy gave her a few more basic instructions and encouragements, but she could tell he was one of the learn-by-doing sort of teachers, so Jenny forced herself to take deep breaths and just get on. He held his hands together to give her a leg up, and she swung her leg over Credo's back awkwardly, almost kicking Easy in the head with her boot. She wriggled in the sleek leather saddle, getting her bearings. "Are you comfortable?" Easy asked, adjusting the stirrups and placing the reins in her hands.

"I feel like I'm riding an elephant," she said with a giddy laugh. Being on a horse made her feel so . . . *tall!*

Easy hopped onto Marymount's horse. "You ready to start moving now?"

Deep breaths, deep breaths. "Yes," Jenny squeaked.

"Then just give Credo a little squeeze with your calves. And just sort of let your hips follow her movements. It'll fall into place." Easy started off on Diana, and Jenny pressed her lower legs gently against Credo's sides. She gasped when Credo started to move.

"Am I trotting?" she asked eagerly.

"Not yet." Easy laughed. "Are you sure you're ready for it?"

Their eyes met across the grass, and he kicked his horse into a trot, pulling away from her quickly. "Come on!" he cried, glancing back over his shoulder, his curls blowing in the light breeze.

"I'll be extra nice to Easy if you're nice to me," she whispered to Credo before squeezing her legs and feeling the horse lurch forward beneath her. "Whoa," she gasped.

An hour later they were back at the stable, Jenny's legs aching with effort. She couldn't believe how much fun it was, riding the enormous, scary-sweet Credo through the fields, even if Jenny wouldn't go faster than a trot, no matter how much Easy encouraged her. The sky was cloudy when they started out, but it quickly darkened, and fat raindrops had begun to fall from the menacing gray clouds. They rode into the stable, which was clean and dark and smelled like Easy, only much more concentrated.

Easy slid off his horse and led her into a stall before returning to Jenny. "Did you like it?" he asked, though he knew the answer from the wild, breathless smile on her face.

"I see what the big deal is now." She unhooked her boot from the stirrup, and dismounted a little more gracefully than she'd mounted. "That was so much fun." Her legs were shaking a little from the strain, and as she pulled off her helmet, she realized her hair felt sweaty and must be plastered to her head, but she didn't care.

"Makes you realize you're alive, doesn't it?" Easy remarked as he pulled off Credo's saddle and hung it on a giant metal hook. He led Credo back into her stall, a huge, straw-filled enclosure.

"It makes me realize other things too," she responded

obliquely, feeling bold. She felt her blood racing through her veins, her adrenaline at an all-time high. On Credo, she felt like she could race across the world, and now, standing on her own two legs again, she felt like she could do whatever she wanted. And what she wanted was to kiss Easy.

"Like what?" He cocked his eyebrows, staring at her. Jenny didn't answer. He was moving closer, ever so slowly. She wanted to capture each individual moment leading up to this. She took in the smells of the stable. The noise of Credo's breathing. The beginnings of rain trammeling against the metal roof. The crunch of straw beneath her boots. The way her legs were shaking. The way Easy touched her on the chin and tilted it upward. And the way he brought his lips toward hers and kissed her, at which moment she stopped thinking about anything at all besides the feeling of kissing the boy she never thought she would ever kiss.

OwlNet

To: RufusHumphrey@poetsonline.com
From: JennyHumphrey@waverly.edu
Date: Sunday, September 15, 6:58 p.m.
Subject: Country living

Dad,

You're not going to believe this, but I went horseback riding today. As in, I rode a horse—an enormous, ten-ton creature with really big teeth. And it wasn't even scary! Well, it was a little scary, but I had an expert helping me along. A very cute expert. But I won't say anything else about that now . . . I don't want to jinx anything.

I'm having fun here—got my first A+, had an assist in the last field hockey game, and have been meeting tons of cool people. It's a little weird not having uniforms to wear to class every day. (It makes it a little harder to get ready in the morning!) I still feel a little like a new girl, trying to figure out all the unspoken rules. But I'm getting the hang of it.

How's the apartment without me and Dan? Is Vanessa around enough to keep you company? Tell her if she wants to paint it orange and fill my closet with the entire Barneys Co-op, that's fine.

I miss you like crazy. Tell Dan he could send his little sister an email once in a while—who knows, maybe she even misses him!

Your favorite daughter,

Jenny

 **OwlNet**

To: EasyWalsh@Waverly.edu
From: EricDalton@waverly.edu
Date: Monday, September 16, 9:45 a.m.
Subject: Meeting

Dear Mr. Walsh,

I apologize for the late notice, but I trust you will receive this in time. Please do me the honor of stopping by my office today before lunch.

Best,

EFD

A WAVERLY OWL KNOWS HIS ADVISER HAS
HIS BEST INTERESTS IN MIND. RIGHT?

You would have thought Easy was two hours late rather than five minutes, judging from the look on Dalton's face when he opened the door. "Sorry I'm late," Easy said, wondering why he seemed to always be apologizing to this guy.

"Sit down." Dalton nodded toward a shiny leather chair while he stood behind his desk, looking like someone in an acting class who had just been instructed to do "stern."

Three hours ago, Easy had been sitting at the conference table in his European history seminar, yawning uncontrollably and taking enormous sips from a triple-shot latte, trying not to think about Jenny. He'd been too wired to sleep last night and had stayed up playing GameCube until three in the morning, so he could barely drag his ass out of bed when the alarm went off at seven. He was impressed with how quickly

Jenny got used to riding Credo. He was afraid that she'd be too terrified to do much more than pet her, but she hopped right on, and even though she looked completely terrified, she managed to trot for almost forty-five minutes. God, she was sweet.

Underneath the table, Easy checked his email on his phone, hoping for a note from Jenny telling him when they'd get together again. But instead, he had only a message from Eric Dalton asking him to come to his office before lunch. What the hell was that about?

He had assumed that Dalton just wanted him to check in since he was still on probation from getting caught in Callie's room after hours. That seemed so long ago now. He didn't even remember that as the night he and Callie had almost done it; he just remembered it as the first time he touched Jenny, when he sat on her bed piss drunk. She had smelled so good—like sleep and oranges and toothpaste—that he wanted to fall asleep next to her.

Easy stared at Dalton. He'd always known the guy was shifty. Easy had seen the way Dalton interacted with girls. Like he couldn't believe his luck, getting to be surrounded by so many gorgeous chicks who fawned over him, completely forgetting that they were off-limits to him. And he'd heard the rumors about him and Brett.

"Easy?" Dalton clasped his hands together and spoke slowly as though he was talking to someone who was a little retarded. "Do you understand what *probation* means?"

Easy pretended not to have heard Dalton's patronizing tone,

wondering if this was some sort of test. Maybe Dalton just needed to feel like a tough guy sometimes. "It means I don't get to make any more mistakes or I'm kicked out."

"Thank you." Dalton leaned back in his chair, his elbows on the arms and his fingers making a temple. "I have to tell you that I've received several reports of you breaking your probation."

"Breaking it?" Easy asked incredulously. "How? I haven't done anything. Who told you I did?"

"We've gotten several reports," Dalton repeated, unfazed, "that you've been skipping classes."

"Oh, yeah? From who?" Easy thought back to the day when he met Jenny out in the woods for the painting project. Her last period was a free period that day, and he'd been so eager to get together with her, he'd skipped his AP Art History lecture. But it was a giant class, held in the Berkman-Meier auditorium in the dark, and Professor Johnson acted like his students thought it was a privilege to be in his lecture and never bothered to take attendance. If the professor didn't bust him, who would have?

"Anonymous." Dalton was clearly acting tough because he knew he had nothing on him. He started to relax a little. "And you can't get expelled on a rumor—that's true. But it's going to mean that you've got another two weeks of in-house suspension, and if you get caught doing anything else wrong, well, I'm not going to be able to help you."

You're the last guy I'd throw a rope to, Easy wanted to say. But he groaned instead, realizing the Boston trip was planned for next weekend. The Ritz, Jenny, Jenny in some kind of sexy costume—it all sounded so great. "I don't get it—this doesn't make any sense. I didn't do anything. Can't you just give me a break?"

"Rules are rules. You knew what *probation* meant. You should have been smarter."

"Rules *are* rules," Easy repeated thoughtfully. "Huh. That sounds funny, coming from you." Easy spoke evenly, watching Dalton's face for a reaction. He took a job at a small private boarding school and within the first week tried to bag one—or more—of the students? In Kentucky, you'd get taken out back and beaten until you understood how to be a gentleman. And here he was, trying to be all disciplinarian and self-righteous. Easy looked at the ERIC DALTON name placard on his desk and realized how easily he could turn the ERIC into PRICK with a little white latex paint.

The room fell completely silent for several long, awkward moments while Easy wondered what Dalton would say. Finally Dalton cleared his throat. "I don't know what you're trying to imply, but if I were you, I'd stop worrying about other people and try to remain focused on not getting expelled."

"Why are you being such a hard-ass?" Dalton clearly had a weird need to feel powerful and knock down some lowly students in his way.

"Why are you being such a dumb-ass? Waverly's the best thing that happened to you, so you better get it together and realize that and stop pissing your future away." It was the kind of thing one of Easy's brothers would say to him, except all three of them were older than Dalton, and even if they treated Easy like a lazy kid, they weren't nearly as condescending as Dalton was. What was this guy's deal, anyway?

"Thanks for the advice, *adviser*." Easy shook his head and stood up to go. "I've got to get to lunch—I don't want any reports to come in that I missed it."

To: CallieVernon@waverly.edu;
BrettMesserschmidt@waverly.edu;
SageFrancis@waverly.edu;
CelineColista@waverly.edu;
BennyCunningham@waverly.edu;
AlisonQuentin@waverly.edu;
JennyHumphrey@waverly.edu;
VerenaArneval@waverly.edu
From: TinsleyCarmichael@waverly.edu
Date: Monday, September 16, 5:43 p.m.
Subject: Le initiation

My dearest Café Society lovelies,

Initiation Evening Pizza Soiree TONIGHT. Essential for all who wish to stay in the society's good graces and attend next weekend's tête-à-tête in Boston. Dumbarton 303, 8 p.m. Be there.

Mr. Pardee, aka Señor Swanky, purchased tickets to the philharmonic tonight. (He sent Mrs. Pardee flowers too—sounds like he's trying to smooth something over!) The happy couple won't be home until well after midnight. Thank you, Sage, for your diligent snooping!

We will be ordering in from our favorite pizza place, Ritoli's, of course.

Please note: Dress code is short, tight, and heart-attack-inducing.

Decadently yours,

T

WHEN IN ROME, A SMART OWL THINKS TWICE
BEFORE DOING AS THE ROMANS DO.

"What do you think the guys do in their club?" Callie poured some vodka into her Waverly mug filled with Country Time lemonade and stirred it with a plastic spoon. She stood at the window where the makeshift bar was set up and stared out at the dark quad, still only half dressed in her black slip skirt and white lace corset. With no makeup on, she looked like a naughty French maid.

"Who knows." Brett flicked her clove cigarette at the gold-trimmed Limoges teacup she was currently using as an ashtray. She missed, and gray ash crumbled onto the floor.

Jenny was flipping through her drawers absentmindedly, occasionally taking a sip from her insulated Waverly cup decorated with maroon and gold owl silhouettes and filled with the spiked lemonade. Dumbarton 303 was, for the first time, as clean as it had been the day they all arrived. The girls had put away all their clothes and books, cleared off their desks, and pushed their beds back against the walls. They propped up pillows, vacuumed, and crisscrossed strings of red Chinese lanterns from the ceiling, purchased that morning from the art store in Rhinecliff. Tinsley's iPod was playing through her "pre-party" playlist.

"All I want to do is have some fun . . ." Sheryl Crow croaked lustily.

"I don't know if I have anything exactly heart-attack-inducing." Jenny turned toward the other girls. *This* was what boarding school was supposed to be like—hanging out with her roommates, drinking spiked lemonade from plastic mugs and ordering pizzas, talking about boys and maybe dancing around a little. She tried to ignore the pit that was forming in her stomach, growing bigger and bigger every time she thought about how she'd lied to Callie and Tinsley about Easy. "What should I wear?"

"Oh, come on," Callie scoffed. "All *you* have to do is show a little cleavage."

"Yeah, *please*." Brett sat up. She was already dressed in a flimsy black C&C tank top that tied above her right shoulder, leaving her left shoulder bare and dramatic looking. "I could have the greatest push-up bra in the world, but there's just not that much to push up."

"Are you kidding me?" Jenny squealed. "You do *not* want these." She pointed to her chest. "Every time I put something on, I have to wonder if it makes me look like a *porn star*. Do you know what I'd give to be able to wear that tank top? Or to not have to wear a bra if I didn't feel like it?" Brett and Callie giggled. "I'd be jiggling all over the place, like a . . . bunch of water balloons."

Callie wrinkled her nose and slipped a pair of dangling jade earrings in her ears. "Ew. That's awful."

"Tell me about it." Jenny decided on a black sleeveless Raves T-shirt with strategically placed cutouts designed to show skin in only the right places. With her short Juicy Couture jean skirt, she felt very punk rock.

"Are you guys almost ready?" Tinsley burst into the room wearing a turquoise tube dress, the kind Jenny always saw in Victoria's Secret catalogs—the ultra-clingy, revealing kind that could only be worn by supermodels and girls lucky enough to have curves in exactly the right spots and not an ounce of fat in any of the wrong spots. Clearly Tinsley was one of those people. Her eyelids were covered in gold shimmer, hoop earrings as big as apples hung from her lobes, and she wore a pair of jeweled Giuseppe Zanotti flat sandals on her feet. Wow. Was she even *human*? Jenny looked at herself and Brett and Callie, all dressed in black, and then back to Tinsley's bright blue dress.

"Nice dress, Tinsley," she heard herself saying. She hadn't said much to Tinsley since, well, she'd met her, but screw it. The spiked lemonade was going to her head, and she was feeling a little brave. So what if Tinsley was the queen of Waverly? *She'd* kissed Easy Walsh!

"Why, thank you." Tinsley gave her a throwaway smile, barely looking at her as she walked over to the floor lamp and tossed a dark purple handkerchief over the light, bathing the room in violet.

"Knock knock." Benny Cunningham pushed through the doorway with Sage Francis right behind her. "Are we late?" She was carrying two bottles of bordeaux in one hand and one of those rabbit-shaped corkscrews in the other. "Courtesy of Daddy Cunningham—he just sent these in a back-to-school care package."

"My father just sends me newspaper clippings," Jenny piped up, forgetting about her new Treo for a second.

Benny smiled at Jenny pityingly. "That sucks." Benny's brunette hair was French-braided down her back, and she was wearing what looked like a scarf wrapped around her chest, showing off her sleek stomach and tiny onyx belly button piercing. "Where should I open these?"

"When did you get that?" Tinsley demanded, pointing at the stomach jewelry, which Jenny thought looked like a tick had nestled into Benny's stomach.

"Oh, this summer . . ."

"To impress a *boy*," Sage said, wrapping her tan arms around Benny's shoulders. Her platinum hair contrasted with Benny's dark locks. "It didn't work." She kissed Benny on the cheek, leaving a mauve smudge.

"Bitch." Benny shrugged Sage off. "Where's the bar?"

"Over here." Callie walked to the window seat that had been designated the beverage area and helped Benny open the wine bottle and pour the wine into the plastic cups Brett had stolen from the library bathroom. "These are for wine shots," Callie joked, taking one of the filled cups and tossing the liquid down her throat.

"Slow down, girl." Benny sipped at her own plastic cup. "Or you're going to end up curled around the toilet tonight."

Soon the other girls arrived, wearing the requisite short, tight outfits and bearing a six-pack of Diet Coke and a bottle of Bacardi Limón. Tinsley had switched the playlist to "party," and the Black Eyed Peas came on. Jenny, Celine, and Brett kicked their shoes in the corner and started dancing. Jenny used to envy the girls who danced like they were practicing to be in someone's music video, but then she realized she could do that too. Suddenly there was a knock at the door. The girls froze, but Tinsley, unafraid, turned the music down a notch and strode over to the door before they could even hide the rum bottle.

The door opened to a welcome sight: Angelo in a pair of well-worn Levi's and a navy blue hooded sweatshirt, holding four boxes of sweet-smelling pizzas. *Hello!*

"You sneak!" Callie cried out, thinking they'd been busted. "I didn't even know you ordered it yet!"

"Thank you, Angelo, for bringing this all the way up here for us. That's very sweet. Could you put them on that table, please?" Tinsley indicated one of the suitcases they had covered with tapestries, and when Angelo headed in that direction, she casually closed the door. Jenny took a deep breath. She had a feeling that in Tinsley's mind, the party was just starting.

"Can I get you a glass of wine? A rum and Coke?" Celine leaned toward Angelo and stroked the neck of the wine bottle suggestively. Was she really trying to win that bet?

"Yeah, um, I don't know if I can really stay." Angelo's eyes wandered around the room, and he shuffled his feet nervously. "I've never been in one of the girls' dorm rooms before. This is pretty sweet."

"You really have to stay for a drink or two." Callie pressed a spare Waverly mug filled with rum and Coke into his hand. "Or else you'll hurt our feelings." He stared at her, transfixed, and took the mug. She grinned triumphantly at Celine, who stuck out her tongue. Jenny couldn't help hoping that maybe Callie would fall madly in love with Angelo. Then she wouldn't mind *who* Easy was with.

"Is this what all your Monday nights are like here?" Angelo sat down on the floor next to another tapestry-covered suitcase. He still looked a little uncomfortable, like he really wanted to call his buddies and have them join him to protect him from the pack of rabid teenage girls.

"Sometimes we order Chinese." Tinsley sat down next to Angelo, holding a paper plate with a gooey slice of mushroom-and-cheese pizza. She leaned back against the bed, and he dragged his eyes away from her and focused on his drink. He took an enormous gulp, wiping his full lips with the back of his hand.

"And sometimes we play games." Callie sat down on the other side of Angelo, leaning into him. "Wanna play a game?"

Poor guy. He was probably thinking, *Who the fuck are all these weird girls?* Jenny was reminded of the scene in *Monty Python and the Holy Grail* (one of her brother's favorite movies, although he was too much of a snob to admit it in front of anyone) where Sir Galahad discovers the castle full of beautiful and lonely nuns, and they pull him inside and practically devour him before he's rescued—to his dismay—by Lancelot. Angelo looked like he knew he was about to be devoured and seemed appropriately freaked out and turned on. He ran a hand through his black hair. "Uh, what kind of game?"

Benny plopped down to her knees in front of him, holding the empty bottle of wine. "Well, we have a bottle. . . ."

"How's that going to work with so many girls?" Alison nudged in next to Benny, sitting cross-legged in a pair of sleek red satin pants. The rest of the girls formed a little circle in the carpet. "I may be drunk, but I'm not making out with you, Benny."

Benny smirked at her. "Why not? You've made out with everyone else."

"How about this?" Tinsley spoke up, as if she'd just come up with a brilliant idea, but Jenny suspected she'd been planning this from the start. "We'll spin the bottle, and whoever it lands on has to kiss Angelo."

Shit, Jenny thought, trying to meet Brett's gaze. She didn't want to kiss Angelo. Was there any way she could get out of here before things got too crazy? Maybe she could pretend to go to the bathroom and just stay there for the rest of the night. But maybe it wouldn't come to that . . . She really didn't want to be a party pooper, not when she was just starting to feel like she finally belonged here.

"I think I need another drink." Angelo rubbed his hand over his eyes and chuckled to himself. Callie got up and poured him another, using a little more rum this time, and gulped down more wine. She walked carefully back to the circle, like she could already feel the room beginning to tilt.

"You do the honors and spin first, Angelo." Tinsley placed the bottle in the middle of the small Oriental area rug that Callie's mother had sent to school with her as a dorm-room-warming gift.

He spun. The fat bottle twirled around and around on the rug before wobbling to a stop, pointing directly at Benny. She gave a squeal of delight and crawled on her knees across the circle, pausing to sit up in front of Angelo, who was staring at her long neck, her hair pulled up into a calculatedly sloppy ponytail.

"Here goes nothing." Benny leaned in and pressed her lips to Angelo's full ones. He seemed shocked at the suddenness of her move, but then he quickly yielded, and all the girls watched as their lips moved together.

Guess Benny wasn't as much of a prude as everyone seemed to think, Jenny thought, a little surprised. Benny finally pulled away and shimmied back to her place in the circle, her lips wet and curled in a huge grin.

"My turn," Callie ordered, jealous that Benny got to kiss Angelo first. She turned the mouth of the bottle toward her this time, then grabbed Angelo and kissed him hard and passionately, like she thought they were on a soap opera. Brett nudged Jenny as the kiss stretched on and on. Angelo was about to reach up and touch Callie's hair when Tinsley cleared her throat authoritatively.

"Sorry." Callie pulled away, keeping her eyes glued to Angelo, who looked like he wished the game were over so he could kiss Callie exclusively. Next Brett spun the bottle sloppily, and Jenny's heart dropped when it wobbled to a stop between her and Verena, but clearly closer to Jenny.

"So close!" Verena exclaimed in disappointment. "Go ahead, Jenny, it's you."

"Yeah, but it's in the middle." Cute as Angelo was, the idea of making out with anyone besides Easy made Jenny feel sick. There was no way she could do what Callie had done now that she'd kissed Easy. It just seemed gross to kiss any other guy.

"What's the matter, Jenny? Don't you want to play?" Tinsley smiled. "Verena will get her turn, don't worry."

Jenny could feel everyone watching her. And all of a sudden the dim purplish light in the room seemed kind of freaky. Callie's eyes seemed to be piercing through her. Shit. Shit. *Shit.* Callie was going to know something was up if she refused to play along.

With her heart in her throat, Jenny crawled over to Angelo, her bare knees getting rug burn. She paused in front of him. He still looked a little bewildered but had clearly decided to just go with it. Quickly she pressed her lips to his cheek and scooted back.

"Don't insult us. Real kisses only, please." Tinsley leaned forward, her hair falling around her face like a curtain, her violet eyes like lasers. "It's not like there's someone else, right?"

As always, Tinsley's voice was light and seemingly carefree, but Jenny knew enough to realize that this was a test—if she didn't do it right, she might as well kiss her dreams of belonging to the intimate world of the Waverly elite goodbye. And that was all she ever wanted, wasn't it? To be one of the pretty, popular girls, friends with someone like Tinsley Carmichael. That was priceless—surely she could trade off one small, teeny-tiny kiss on the lips for that?

Without saying anything, Jenny abruptly turned to Angelo again, and, before she could stop herself, kissed him full on the mouth. She'd intended to just hold her lips there for a sufficient amount of time, but Angelo was clearly getting into the game, and she felt his tongue pry open her lips and find its way into her mouth. She forced herself to count to three before pulling away and retreating back to her spot in the circle, barely resisting the urge to grab Brett's jumbo bottle of Scope from her dresser to gargle.

Jenny glanced at Tinsley, hoping to see some sign of acceptance in her eyes, but they didn't look any different than they had thirty seconds ago.

"Don't forget to spin," Tinsley said coolly, leaning against the bed with her arms crossed in front of her chest, looking like a queen who had just seen a mediocre performance by one of her underlings and was now ready for the next thing. She nudged the bottle toward Jenny with her toe.

Suddenly Jenny realized with a horrible sinking feeling, as if the elevator she was in had just dropped twenty floors, that gaining Tinsley's approval wasn't going to be as simple as making out with the pizza boy.

Jenny spun the bottle blindly, and as the game continued, she had to bite the insides of her cheeks to keep herself from spilling tears like the big baby she was. What had she done? She was disgusted with herself—how could she let Tinsley push her around like that? And how could she do this to Easy? She couldn't wait to brush her teeth and get the horrible taste of another guy out of her mouth.

"Who's up for a game of strip poker?" Callie staggered to her feet, the heel of her satin Kate Spade pump piercing a half-eaten piece of pizza lying on the floor. "Fuck." She slid her foot out of the shoe, leaving it where it was.

"Will you stay and play with us, Angelo?" Sage sat down next to him and draped her arm around his shoulders, bitter that she hadn't gotten a chance to kiss him but willing to trade for the opportunity to see him strip.

"I guess I could stay a while longer."

"Hey." Brett nudged Jenny, looking concerned. "Wanna get out of here? We can watch TV in the lounge or something."

Jenny clutched Brett's arm gratefully, feeling drunk and depressed and badly in need of some downtime. "God, please. Let's go." Brett stood up and pulled Jenny to her feet.

"Where are you going?" Callie demanded, rummaging through her desk drawer for the pack of cards she kept there.

Brett stretched her back and yawned. "We're going to head down to the lounge and watch a movie. I'm really drunk. If I have any more, I'll be sick. I'm not much of a card player anyway." She picked up a paper plate and loaded a few slices of pizza on it before scooting out the door behind Jenny, who looked like she was about to cry. "See ya."

Callie slammed the drawer shut and narrowed her eyes. Brett didn't look drunk, though Jenny certainly did. What were they thinking, leaving the Café Society meeting before anything really good had happened?

"Brett has gotten *so* boring." Tinsley shuffled the cards like a pro. Tinsley handed the cards to Celine, who dealt them, giggling the whole time and nudging Angelo, who was looking quite drunk. Sage took the tortoiseshell clip from Celine's hair and stuck it in Angelo's head. They all collapsed into drunken giggles.

"She's been bitchy all year," Callie said, bitter at Brett for having rejected her company yet again. "And she's bummed that Mr. Dalton lost interest." Callie picked up someone's half-full mug and downed it. She knew she was getting plastered, but it distracted her from feeling sorry for herself. Why were Brett and Jenny getting so cliquey without her? What made *them* so chummy? She wouldn't have minded curling up on one of the couches downstairs with her cashmere blanket and a bag of Cheetos and watching a Lindsay Lohan movie with the two of them, *if* they'd thought to invite her.

"About that . . ." Tinsley leaned in confidentially. "I might know the reason for the sudden change in his affections."

"You?" Callie tried not to look horrified. She glanced around. Benny and Alison were pouring more drinks and not paying attention, and Verena and Celine and Sage were completely wrapped up in Angelo.

Tinsley nodded her glossy head. "Yeah. We had a very . . . *promising* meeting last week. And he's taking me to New York tomorrow for a little romantic getaway." She grinned proudly.

Callie had to look away. How could Tinsley *do* that? And what about Mr. Dalton? How many students was he going to try and sleep with? Poor Brett. Of course Tinsley was to blame. Callie shivered, wondering if she should go down and talk to Brett right now. But then, she was undoubtedly too busy with her *new* best friend, Jenny.

Instead, she poured herself another drink. Tinsley was horrible, yes, but at least she was open about it. Callie couldn't help feeling like Brett and Jenny were just as bad . . . just more secretive. But maybe it was just the wine talking. Maybe.

**OwlNet**   Email Inbox

To: Eric Dalton's students and advisees
From: EricDalton@waverly.edu
Date: Tuesday, September 17, 8:55 a.m.
Subject: No class today

Dear Students,

Due to unexpected circumstances, I won't be able to attend class today. Please continue with the scheduled assignments from the syllabus. Thank you—I'll see you tomorrow.

Sincerely,

EFD

To: CallieVernon@waverly.edu
From: BrandonBuchanan@waverly.edu
Date: Tuesday, September 17, 9:17 a.m.
Subject: U sick?

Hey, Callie,

I'm in Latin, but you're not here. Just wanted to see if you want me to bring you soup or an almond croissant . . . or Gatorade?

Love,
Brandon

TO AVOID A HANGOVER, A WAVERLY OWL

MUST STAY HYDRATED.

Callie woke up with a headache like a car wreck and her mouth tasting like sawdust. She peeked out from under her cashmere blanket and was greeted by hot, blinding sunlight. What time was it? She had to pee, but any movement sent alarm sirens through her head, and she wasn't sure she wanted to leave her snuggly burrow to face the day. Her stomach was roiling—how much had she had to drink? She had a vague memory of stealing other people's plastic cups of wine and Waverly mugs filled with rum and Cokes. The smell of rum coming from a mug on the floor made her stomach lurch, even though it was empty. She remembered spending a few hours in the bathroom, vomiting up everything in her stomach, which was really just alcohol since she'd skipped the pizza. No wonder her mouth was so dry. She had to get some water or she'd die. What time was it, anyway? Today was Tuesday, right? She was sure she was missing some class, but it hurt her head to try to think of which one.

She kicked off her blanket, revealing an empty, sun-dappled room. Pizza boxes still lay on the floor. She reached for her cell phone and turned it on. Next to it, on her nightstand, stood an Evian bottle and two Tylenol capsules. Tinsley. Tears came to her eyes. Tinsley never managed to get as drunk as anyone else and always managed to remember the water. An image from last night came back to her—Tinsley holding back her blond hair as she knelt over the toilet. Callie had been a stumbling, swearing, crying, sweaty mess, and Tinsley had sat with her in the bathroom, making her drink water and holding her hair back when she was sick. Tinsley had listened to her wail about Easy for hours, just reassuring her things would be okay and that he'd get what he deserved.

She loved that girl, even if she had stolen Mr. Dalton from Brett. That was totally insane. But none of her business, really. Let Brett and Tinsley duke it out; it had nothing to do with her. Callie cracked open the bottle of water and washed down the Tylenol before collapsing back on her pillow with her phone in hand. 10:29 A.M. She pulled her covers back over her head, shutting out the annoying sunlight. She had seven new text messages. At least one of them could be from Easy, right? Her thumb clicked down through them. Five from Brandon. Two from Angelo—when had she given him her number? Probably when she had her tongue down his throat. What was wrong with her?

Maybe because she only wanted one person and he wasn't interested. Callie dialed his number anyway, feeling safe beneath her covers. Maybe he'd just needed some time apart? Maybe he missed her? But his phone didn't even ring, just went directly to voice mail: "This is Easy. Leave me a message." The only thing worse than leaving a hungover message on an ex-boyfriend's voice mail was leaving a drunken one, and she was grateful that Tinsley had taken away her phone last night; otherwise she probably would have tried that too.

She flipped her phone shut before the beep and pressed her face into her pillow. Maybe she could just sleep through this day. Or this year.

A WAVERLY OWL DOES NOT
KISS AND TELL.

Jenny wandered around campus on Tuesday morning, so overcome with guilt that she couldn't sit still. She'd been unable to sleep last night, even after Brett had gotten her out of there and the two of them had giggled and watched *The 40-Year-Old Virgin* in the lounge. But Jenny was still tormented by how she had idiotically let Tinsley goad her into making out with Angelo. It made her sick just thinking about it. What had she done?

Part of her had wanted to hide under her scratchy baby-blue blanket all day, but then she felt like she was going to suffocate breathing the same air as Callie and Tinsley. Now she was outside on the quad, but she still felt the same stifling bubble around her head. If she didn't get away from here, she was seriously going to flip out. She pulled out her new Treo and dialed the one person she knew could make her feel better.

"Muffulupugus!" Rufus's deep baritone rumbled loudly through her new phone. His voice made her smile, even though she had to hold her cell phone away from her ear. "How the hell are you?"

"I'm . . . I'm good, Dad." Jenny tugged at a long curl of hair. "I was just kind of hoping you could maybe call the Waverly office and get them to give me a mental health day."

"A what? A mental health day? Are you all right?" Great, make him worry about you getting kicked out of another school.

"I just need an afternoon in the city, but I won't do any shopping, just go to a couple of museums. You'll meet me. We'll get fried dough at the Mexican place on Amsterdam."

"No can do, sweets. I'm assisting Vanessa on a film this afternoon. . . . There's this hugely overweight squirrel in Bryant Park. We want to capture what it eats in an entire twenty-four-hour period, except we're kind of cheating. Anyway, you're still doing all right there?" Rufus sounded worried. "I thought you were enjoying it—the A's, the field hockey, the horseback riding?"

"I'm doing great, I swear." Jenny crossed her fingers as she lied. "I just miss the city—it gets a little suffocating . . . being out here with all this fresh air. I think I might be getting too much oxygen or something."

He sighed heavily, but Jenny could tell he couldn't resist. "All right. I'll call the office and tell them I need you home for the day."

Jenny squealed and thanked him profusely. The second she hung up, she called a cab to meet her at the front gate and practically skipped back to the dorm to grab her wallet.

Suddenly Waverly didn't feel suffocating now that she knew she could get away from it for the day. Yeah, she'd screwed up, but with any luck, Easy wouldn't find out about it, and it really *was* just a little kiss. Plus it wasn't like she and Easy were dating . . . not officially. She couldn't wait to catch the next train out of this incestuous world and into the big, wonderful city.

"Jenny!" She whirled around to see Easy jogging across the grassy quad toward her, and her skin tingled. His long legs caught up to her easily. He looked extra cute in a pair of dark brown cords—she'd never seen him in anything other than Levi's—and a plain white T-shirt. "Where are you running off to?"

"Oh, um, I'm going to the city for the day. . . . I need to breathe, you know, polluted air." Jenny felt herself fidgeting, convinced that Easy could see right through her. She tapped her red boot against the grass.

"Yeah, this much fresh air can't be good for a city kid." A dark curl flopped in front of his eyes and he blew it out of the way. "Waverly can feel like it's got this giant bubble over it, and you forget sometimes that nothing here is really life or death."

"*Exactly.*" Jenny smiled. "Hey, do you . . . want to come with me?" she asked impulsively. Although she had been fantasizing about wandering through the vast halls of the Met by herself, suddenly the picture seemed so much more complete if Easy was in it too. And maybe if she could be alone with him in the real world, the things that had happened last night in the Waverly bubble wouldn't matter so much. "We could get lunch, maybe go to a couple of museums."

"Yeah?" Easy looked at Jenny's face with eagerness, then

frowned in disgust. "I'm on, like, double probation from Dalton. And since I don't know who his spies are, I don't know if I can risk pissing him off more."

Jenny's face fell. "I totally forgot about that. Oh, well, the last thing I want is for you to get kicked out of here—"

"Except . . ." Easy interrupted Jenny and smiled at her. "Dalton sent out an email this morning saying he was sick. So presumably he's not around. . . . Let's go."

Jenny's brown eyes widened. "But . . ."

He grabbed her hand, and the feel of his warm, rough fingers against her skin silenced her.

The train to the city was crowded, but Jenny and Easy found two seats together, playing tic-tac-toe in her sketchbook and each listening to Easy's iPod with one headphone until they pulled into Grand Central Station. They took a cab uptown to the Met, but before going in, Easy bought them each a hot dog from a sidewalk vendor and they sat on the steps of the museum in the early-autumn sunshine. She'd done this so many times, hoping that one of the cools girls like Blair or Serena would notice her or that someone famous might sit down next to her and suddenly she'd show up in *Us Weekly* as the mysterious companion of some famous A-list actor.

Jenny leaned back against the stone steps and sighed. For years, all she'd wanted was to be one of those girls people talked about. When Socrates said that an "unexamined life" wasn't worth living, Jenny totally agreed—so what if he was talking about *personally* examining your life and not, like, Page Six examining. It meant the same to her. She knew it was shallow, but she couldn't help it. All of literature was filled with the sort of devastatingly beautiful and seductive women whose image became tattooed on the brain of everyone in the room, making them smile or groan in anguish when they thought of her, which they inevitably would. Flaky Daisy Buchanan from *The Great Gatsby*. Lily Bart from *The House of Mirth*. Petrarch's Laura, Dante's Beatrice. She didn't want anyone to write a book about her necessarily—but she wanted to be the kind of person that *could* inspire someone to do that. Was that so wrong?

But now, sitting here with Easy, she suddenly didn't care if she was the kind of girl Jay Gatsby would remember years later, or Heath Ferro, or Tinsley crazy-scary-bitch Carmichael. Or if she ever showed up on Page Six again. All that mattered was Easy sitting next to her in one of her most-favorite spots in the world, with a small blob of ketchup on his cheek.

"Waverly's definitely a small place. Especially when you start out like you did—with a big splash." He took another bite of hot dog. "But people would have known you right away anyway."

Jenny wiped the ketchup away with her thumb. "Why do you say that?" She nervously thought of her chest—not too many of Waverly's pedigreed cashmere-cable-knit-sweater-and-tweed-Theory-skirt crowd had the double D's she sported. She definitely did not want any sonnets written for her boobs.

Easy swallowed. "Because . . . I don't know, it sounds stupid . . . but you've got this *sparkle*."

"*Me?*" She looked down at the cement steps, feeling a little shy but totally flattered.

Easy just smiled and requested a "Jenny Humphrey highlights tour" through the museum. They ended up winding back through the galleries several times, looking for the things Jenny loved the most—a Cézanne painting with dozens of apples spilling across a table, the pink Klimt portrait of a pretty young girl that Jenny had always wished was her, the quiet Vermeer of a young woman holding a water pitcher, the misty George Inness of a single girl wandering through an orchard, the beautifully calligraphied Islamic manuscripts. Easy paused in front of each one, silently taking it in and then kissing her.

She knew she'd never see the same pieces of art in the same way again. They were more than her favorite paintings now. They were part of her most-perfect day ever.

24

A WAVERLY OWL KNOWS HOW TO KEEP A SECRET,

EVEN A JUICY ONE.

"I wish I didn't have to give it back," Tinsley pouted. She set down her lychee martini on the bar's glass top and slid the antique bracelet over her hand. "But thank you for letting me borrow it."

"My pleasure." Eric smiled at her, and she held his gaze. They'd arrived at the hotel an hour earlier and taken a seat at the sleek hotel bar while the concierge had their bags sent to their suite. They were already on to their third martini, although they weren't yet on their first kiss. "Now. Here's to—"

"Secrets," Tinsley interrupted. After their flirtatious emails, she'd assumed they'd rip each other's clothes off and do it in the back of Eric's limo as soon as he picked her up. Instead, he'd asked her to tell him stories about her family and told her about his father and the stick up his ass. So far, the day together had been remarkably *un*sexy. She was ready to change all that, though. "Who doesn't like a good secret?"

Eric leaned toward her. "Well . . . I know I do."

There. That was a little better. "You must have some good ones," Tinsley goaded him. For some reason, she wanted to hear him tell her that he liked Brett but how that had changed the minute he laid eyes on *her*. She wanted to hear how much smarter and sexier and cooler she was.

"Me? Nah." He sat back, taking another sip from his glass. The bartender switched the music to some sultry jazz, as though he'd been reading her mind. "Though I'm sure *you* do."

"Hmmm . . ." She pretended to think. If he wasn't going to come out with it, she could help him along. "Well, I have this friend, Brett. . . ."

Eric cleared his throat. A six-foot model Tinsley recognized from last year's Blumarine fashion show walked into the bar, but Eric didn't take his eyes off her. "Tinsley, I—"

"So it's not *my* secret, exactly," she went on, prying her eyes away from the model. "But she told everyone at Waverly her family saves puffins or something in Newfoundland, even though her dad is actually a liposuction specialist in New Jersey! Can you *believe*?"

"She mentioned that once." Eric looked around the dimly lit room nervously. "So I guess that's not such a big secret."

Wait, *what*? That was Brett's biggest secret ever, and she'd told Eric? Eric *Dalton*? Tinsley was suddenly seized with a panicky feeling that maybe there was more to his fling with

Brett than she'd thought. Maybe he *didn't* think she was sexier and more beautiful than Brett. "I didn't realize you were so close," she murmured coldly.

"Don't be like that," he scolded her, which she was surprised to enjoy. She felt suddenly like the naughty schoolgirl that she was. He reached over, cupped her chin in his hand, and met her gaze. "I'm sure people must tell you this all time, but you have the most *beautiful* eyes."

And with that, he leaned in to kiss her. As their lips met, she couldn't help but think that yes, people *did* tell her that all the time. She was forever waiting for someone to tell her that the beauty mark hidden behind her ear was the sexiest thing he'd ever seen, but so far, no one had ever even noticed it. But as Eric slipped his hand down her neck and fingered the opening of her delicate navy wrap dress, she swept her thick dark hair behind her. She might as well give him the *chance* to see it, right?

"Should we check out our suite?" he whispered breathily.

"Let's do that."

A GOOD OWL DOES NOT SCHEME . . . ALTHOUGH A NAUGHTY OWL JUST MIGHT.

By early evening, Jenny and Easy were nestled into a cozy table at Balthazar, a posh and bustling Soho brasserie where the waiter didn't bat an eyelash when they ordered a carafe of pinot noir. Jenny leaned back on the red leather bench seat, enjoying the way Easy looked next to her in the high-ceilinged, dark, oak-paneled room. The tables were close together and filled with well-dressed hipsters enjoying aperitifs and gearing up for a night on the town. A giant, antique Parisian brasserie mirror hung above their heads. They ordered a plate of steak frites. Jenny sipped her glass of wine.

"I'm going to run outside and check my messages. Make sure Dalton hasn't called to check up on me or anything." He rolled his eyes. "I'll be right back. Don't eat all the fries without me, okay?"

"I'm not promising anything." Jenny touched her hair,

making sure her barrettes hadn't fallen out, or it would be a mass of frizzies. "I dream about these fries."

"I'll hurry." He gave her a quick kiss on the lips. She was so kissable! It was nice to get off campus for once and to be alone with Jenny without having to worry about Callie hearing about it. He made his way through the tiny spaces between the crowded tables, thinking how nice it would be if he and Jenny could go to a real Parisian brasserie. His heart pounded as he started to think of her in his parents' Parisian garret apartment, lying on the small French bed, completely naked.

As he stepped into the busy Soho street, throngs of evening shoppers bounded down the street carrying Bloomingdale's signature brown paper bags and sleek black Barneys Co-op shopping bags. It took him a moment to recognize the girl standing in front of him, wearing a bohemian-looking long-belted cashmere cardigan over a navy blue chiffon wrap dress that was on the verge of unwrapping.

Easy imagined the look on his face to be similar to the shocked one on Tinsley's when she turned around and saw him. What the hell was she doing here? Tinsley quickly regained her composure, however, and pulled the cigarette out of her grinning red lips. "Thought you were on probation."

Easy stared at her and in a flash of memory recalled seeing Tinsley when he and Jenny walked out of the woods together. So she *had* seen. "Are you going to tell on me again?"

Tinsley narrowed her carefully made up eyes. She took another drag on her cigarette and thought for a moment, determined to choose her words carefully. "I know you're here with Jenny. I see her inside. But you know what?" Tinsley's face quickly assumed a self-satisfied expression, and Easy clenched his fist in his pocket. "Jenny just hooked up with somebody else last night. How's that for a sweet little girlfriend?"

Wait, *what*? For a minute, Easy's stomach fell, but then he realized where this information was coming from—scheming Tinsley, bitter that she wasn't the one everyone was talking about at the moment. "Fuck you. I don't believe anything you have to say." He pulled the door open to go back inside. "You've got some real issues, you know that?"

"I'm not the only one." Tinsley smiled sweetly at him, a smile that made his toes curl.

Making his way back to Jenny, Easy forced himself to calm down. He just wanted to enjoy the rest of the day and forget about that jealous bitch outside. Of course she'd say something like that about Jenny. She was sweet and kind and honest—three qualities one would *never* attribute to Tinsley.

"Quick, sit down." Jenny grabbed Easy's hand and pulled him into the booth. "Look!" Easy turned his head and looked out the window, expecting to see Tinsley's lying eyes staring back at them. Instead, he caught a glimpse of Tinsley walking down Spring Street on someone's arm. *Dalton.* "Do you think they saw us?" Jenny asked, clearly worried about Easy's probation.

Easy nodded, still staring out the window. "They may have seen us, but I have an idea." An idea he was definitely going to use to take Dalton down.

26

A WAVERLY OWL MUST REPORT ANY

INAPPROPRIATE FACULTY BEHAVIOR.

Easy always looked forward to his Wednesday morning Advanced French Literature, but today it was because it was the one class he shared with Brett Messerschmidt, and he needed her help. He had to get Dalton busted before Dalton got him *expelled*. Enter Brett. She was class prefect. If she accused Dalton of something, everyone would listen.

Madame Claubert stood at the front of the room, her long gray hair pulled into a clip at the back of her head. She was one of those older women whose beauty just seemed to sharpen and intensify with age. Her cheekbones were perfectly chiseled, her neck long and swanlike, her body as taut as a ballerina's. French women were so sexy.

"Monsieur Walsh, *entrez*." She stood inside the door, waiting to close it.

"*Bien sûr, madame.*" Easy scooted inside and slid into the empty desk in front of Brett. She gave him her typical raised eyebrow half smile. Her skin had more color to it than it had for most of the past week.

"Thank you for joining us. Now we may get started." She held a stack of papers and passed them out to each row. "Please pair up and answer the ten questions in this *examen petit.*" She clapped her thin hands together. "*Dix minutes.*"

Easy spun around in his chair. "Mademoiselle Messerschmidt. Will you do me the honor?"

"*Mais oui.*" Brett was wearing an army green sweater that made her eyes glow greener and a khaki skirt that came to midthigh. She looked totally cute and completely young and innocent. Easy could see why Dalton would be attracted to her, but how could he be slimy enough to act on it?

"Listen . . . ," Easy said when they had answered half the questions. He glanced at her sideways, trying to be subtle. He didn't want to embarrass her or anything. "I heard stuff. . . . But did anything ever actually happen between you and Mr. Dalton?"

Brett's jaw dropped, revealing a platinum filling in one of her bottom molars that Easy had never noticed before. She pulled herself together quickly and gave Easy a withering glare that looked more defensive than angry. "Go to hell."

"No, no, I'm not trying to get you in trouble or anything," Easy said quickly, his fingers twirling his fountain pen. "You know I wouldn't do that."

Brett eyed him suspiciously. What did he want, then? He

looked so eager. Easy wasn't normally much of a gossip. She bit her lip and pretended to scan the list of questions as Madame Claubert left the classroom. "So why are you asking?"

"You're probably not going to enjoy hearing this, but I ran into Tinsley in Soho yesterday." He paused. "She was with Mr. Dalton."

Brett let the words make their way to her brain slowly. She felt sick as their meaning registered. She *knew* it. She knew Tinsley was wearing Eric's platinum link bracelet that night. How could she *do* that? Why? And Eric—she'd meant so little to him that the second Tinsley strutted along, he'd dropped her like last year's Prada pumps? She was such an *idiot*.

"What . . . *jerks*." Brett couldn't think of anything stronger to say. The image of the two of them in bed in the penthouse at the Soho Grand filled Brett with rage. What if she'd actually lost her virginity to Eric? Then suddenly all of her confusion quickly metamorphosed into pure fury. He had lied to her. He didn't think what they were doing was unethical—he just wanted to be doing it with Tinsley. "He should be arrested."

"There's really no way to prove they're together, though. Just because they were in New York together doesn't mean . . ." He sighed.

"It *does* mean that to anyone who knows Tinsley." Brett fiddled nervously with the tiny gold hoops in her ear. The ones Eric had kissed so sweetly. It was all part of his act, she thought angrily.

Easy slumped in his chair. "And I wouldn't want you to have to go public with your ordeal. I'm sure you've been through enough already."

The thought of having to tell the administration—in detail—what had happened between her and Eric—Mr. Dalton, whatever—made her feel totally sick. She shook her head. "Yeah, I don't think I could do that."

Easy shrugged. "Then we've got to get him on something else."

Madame Claubert opened the classroom door. *"Vite! Vite!"* she yelled jovially. *"Deux minutes!"*

Brett tossed her hair and flipped through her copy of *Le Rouge et le Noir*. "Wait a second . . ." She dropped the book on her desk and clutched at Easy's arm. "The time I was at his house, he had a bag of weed on his dresser. Maybe we can use that?"

"But you couldn't tell Marymount where you saw it." Easy drummed his fingers on the wooden desk. "Unless . . ."

"Unless . . ." Brett continued, following Easy's train of thought. "I say I went to his house to pick up some DC files and he offered to *smoke* it with me. . . . I can say exactly where it is in his house, and . . ."

Easy nodded, finishing her sentence: "And what's Dalton going to say to that? He didn't offer it to you, that you just saw it in his bedroom when you happened to be spending the night?"

Brett's lips formed a giddy smile. "He wouldn't risk denying it and having me come out with the truth. Can you imagine, a Dalton being charged with statutory rape?"

Easy looked like he could have hugged her. "He'll be forced to resign."

For the first time since the whole Eric Dalton saga began, she felt like she was in control. "Exactly."

After French class, Easy gave Brett a good-luck pat on the back. She smiled bravely at him and marched directly to Marymount's office in Stansfield Hall. Marymount's secretary, Mr. Tomkins, a balding man who wore only floral ties, was sitting behind an oak desk when Brett walked in. "Hello, Brett dear." Adults always seemed to like Brett, and Mr. Tomkins treated her like she was the bright spot in his day. "What can I do for you?"

Brett straightened her shoulders and said in her most businesslike voice, "I'd like to speak with Dean Marymount, please."

Mr. Tomkins's hand hesitated above the intercom as he prepared to buzz the dean. "What shall I tell him this is about?"

"It's confidential." Brett smiled apologetically. *But not for long.*

27

A THOUGHTFUL OWL IS NEVER UNKIND
TO THOSE LESS FORTUNATE.

After Signor Giraldi finally released Tinsley's advanced Italian class from their torturous lecture about the history of the Petrarchan sonnet, Tinsley strode across the quad, the heels of her Moschino suede T-strap pumps stabbing into randomly scattered early-fallen leaves. She'd only returned from her date with Dalton a few hours ago, and she could still feel his lips on her neck. Even if she hadn't been able to shock him with Brett's Jersey girl secret, well, she had certainly done her part for Callie. It would only be a matter of hours before Easy would be called into Dean Marymount's office to find Eric sitting there with a report that Easy had been in New York yesterday. Callie would never have to see Easy again, and barftastically sweet Jenny would get exactly what she deserved. Tinsley had to bite the inside of her cheek to keep from smiling at the heady rush of power she felt. Tinsley Carmichael was *back*.

She felt a pair of familiar eyes on her and turned to see a shaggy blond-haired boy sprawled lazily on the steps of the chapel. A slow grin spread across Heath Ferro's face when he noticed that he'd gotten her attention. Tinsley immediately changed direction and sauntered toward the chapel, enjoying the way Heath stared at her in her deep V-necked Renaissance-print Cynthia Steffe dress. The fine Italian silk fluttered against her skin, and Heath's eyes followed the sway of her hips as she strode up to him and placed her right foot on the bottom step. "What's up, Ferro?"

"Just enjoying the scenery." Heath stretched his arms into the air. He wore an artfully distressed tee with the word SUPERMAN emblazoned across it.

Tinsley flicked a perfect pale pink nail, coated in Oh, Behave polish, against his cheek. "Like your shirt."

"Sit down," Heath offered, patting his lap.

"Nice try." Tinsley perched daintily on the step above Heath, her bare knees adjacent to his face. He stared at them for a moment before scooting over to make room for her.

"Are plans under way for this weekend?" she asked.

"Ah, this weekend . . . but of course!" Heath smacked his lips and rubbed his hands together. "I took the liberty of reserving two of the Boston Ritz's connecting club-level presidential suites. Views of the gardens from the king-size Jacuzzi."

"Mmmm. Sounds delish. I'll have to pack my bikini."

"Or not." Heath shrugged. "Up to you."

Tinsley smirked at him. "You'd like that, wouldn't you?"

"Do you need to ask?" Heath yawned and closed his eyes,

obviously picturing Tinsley naked in a bubbling tub of steaming hot water, her long dark hair piled on top of her head.

Tinsley slapped him with the back of her hand. "Can you think about something other than me naked for five minutes?" she demanded, pleased, as always, with Heath's flattery.

"Only with great difficulty."

Tinsley leaned toward him and lowered her voice. "Who do you think's going to hook up this weekend?"

"Besides you and me?"

Tinsley rolled her eyes. "Enough."

Heath fingered the SUPERMAN on his chest. "The obvious answer is Easy and little Miss Boobs." He was a little bitter that he'd only gotten to drunkenly kiss Jenny—and that he barely remembered. He wouldn't mind getting his hands on that hot little body of hers. "If they haven't already, that is."

"Well, I've got some juice on her." Tinsley smiled. "Did you know she was making out with someone who definitely was *not* Easy on Monday night?" That girl irked her. Everyone thought she was so nice, with her sweet little smile and blushing pink cheeks, but jumping all over Callie's boyfriend the second they broke up? How nice was that? She hadn't seen Callie since getting back, but she knew she'd have to tell her about bumping into Easy and Jenny in New York once she did.

"Oh, yeah?" Heath rubbed his hands together conspiratorially. "That's interesting."

"Who else?" Tinsley asked, pleased to have planted the seed of a rumor that was sure to blossom into a full-fledged scandal.

"I don't know. . . . Ryan Reynolds wants to make a move on Brett—he thinks he's got a decent shot."

"In hell, maybe," Tinsley scoffed. "She's not *that* desperate."

"Speaking of desperate." Heath nodded in the direction of the quad. Brandon Buchanan headed toward them in a pair of Theory chalk-striped wool trousers and a heather gray Zegna polo beneath his neatly pressed maroon school blazer.

"Don't you guys look suspicious." He paused in front of them. "Discussing government secrets?"

"Close. Talking about this weekend." Heath pulled a pack of cigarettes out from one of the side pockets of his Allen B. cargo pants.

Brandon turned toward Tinsley. "How's Callie doing, by the way?"

Tinsley eyed him suspiciously. "She's fine." When was he going to get over it already? "Great, in fact."

Brandon balanced his shiny gray Salvatore Ferragamo ankle boot on the bottom step. He was probably the only boy at Waverly who actually polished his shoes regularly. Freak. Brandon was an über-metrosexual, with his perfectly stylish wardrobe and the utter invisibility of his pores, something that was not natural in a guy. No wonder Callie had ditched him for Easy Walsh, an über-*sexual* if Tinsley had ever seen one. What did that make Heath? Just plain sexual?

"I haven't seen her around." Brandon bent down and rubbed a smudge of dirt off his shoe.

"Yeah, well." Tinsley shrugged. "She's been busy."

"She hasn't been at the dining hall lately. Is she not eating again?" How cute for Brandon to worry about Callie's well-being. Although she *had* gotten way too skinny.

But before she could respond, Heath burst out laughing. He grabbed Tinsley's arm in mock anguish and cried, "You must tell me! Has she been taking her multivitamins? *Has she been doing her biology homework?*" Heath collapsed into giggles. "You sound like her fucking mother!"

Brandon glared at him angrily. "Fuck off, Heath. So, how many rooms did you get at the Ritz?" he asked casually, changing the subject.

"Two presidential suites."

"You think that'll be enough room for everyone?" Brandon frowned. "Aren't there, like, ten or twelve people going? Where will they all sleep?"

Heath jumped up and did a dance with his hips, as if he were trying to balance a hula hoop around them. "Where will they all sleep?" he repeated in a falsetto, cracking Tinsley up. "Bro, there's not going to be too much sleeping going on if I can help it."

Brandon rolled his eyes. "Maybe I'll get a private room. For me and Callie."

"Why? So you can go watch *The Notebook*? *50 First Dates?*" Heath burst out laughing again. "*Jerry Maguire?* Dude, it's a fucking *party*."

Tinsley giggled. Heath *had* to be the next boy on the Café Society make-out list. Maybe Callie thought he was gross, but he was ten thousand times more fun than Brandon. He would be such a good time, and he'd be *psyched*. Tinsley zoned out while Brandon and Heath continued to squabble like girls. Freshmen on their way across the quad stared at her in awe as she stretched out her legs and yawned. It felt good to be back. But one girl in particular was staring at her so intensely . . . Oh, hell. It was that practically albino Yvonne girl, the one in Tinsley's Italian class who always tried to work with her when they had to pair off. Thankfully, Tinsley was generally skilled at avoiding people, and she cursed herself for not pretending she hadn't seen Yvonne because she was walking over.

Yvonne headed toward them, in a white button-down shirt and pair of navy blue chinos from J.Crew with little green frogs sprinkled across them—the kind of pants that were meant to be worn with a sense of irony, something Yvonne didn't possess.

"Hi, Tinsley," she squeaked, unable to look directly at her. Tinsley felt Yvonne's eyes on her forehead instead. Tinsley gave her a short, cursory smile that encouraged her to keep on walking.

But Yvonne didn't catch it or else was just too determined to speak. "Everyone's been talking about your, um, Boston trip. I was wondering who was going? Like, whole dorms? Can anyone go?"

Tinsley felt Brandon and Heath watching her and could tell Heath was holding back his snickers. Really, what was this girl thinking? That Tinsley would gush, "Oh, yes, come along with us, and be sure to bring all your jazz band/math club friends." Tinsley tried to take the have-you-lost-your-mind-look off her face and made her voice kinder than she felt, only because this poor girl was so clueless, it would do no good to humiliate her. "Secret societies only. Sorry."

Maybe in another lifetime.

 **OwlNet**

To: Waverly Students
From: DeanMarymount@waverly.edu
Date: Wednesday, September 18, 3:01 p.m.
Subject: Eric Dalton resignation

Dear Students,

As of today, Eric Dalton has resigned from his position at Waverly.

His Ancient Civilizations history and beginning Latin classes will be taught by other capable members of the department until a suitable replacement can be found. Students should proceed to class as usual tomorrow.

For those students who had Eric Dalton as an adviser, you will be reassigned. Your respective dorm masters will be in touch shortly.

Thank you for your cooperation,

Dean Marymount

OwlNet

Instant Message Inbox

AlisonQuentin: Yikes, can you believe Dalton got the ax? Just listening to him recite Catallus turned me on. . . .

AlanStGirard: If Latin turns you on so much, come over to my room and we'll watch Caligula.

AlisonQuentin: U r soooo gross. . . . That's a porno!

AlanStGirard: It's not porn. It's historical.

OwlNet

Instant Message Inbox

HeathFerro: Heard Dalton got caught smoking opium in the rare books room, naked with his beginning Latin class.

EasyWalsh: Dream on.

HeathFerro: Sounded kind of hot. Speaking of hot, I heard your girl's been getting around.

EasyWalsh: Shut up, dude.

HeathFerro: Serious. Seeerrrreeeuuuus . . .

OwlNet

RyanReynolds: So your boyfriend's gone now . . .
Maybe we can go out sometime?

BrettMesserschmidt: Uh, what? I think you're trying to reach
Tinsley. . . .

RyanReynolds: Maybe both of you would be interested???

BrettMesserschmidt: Don't write to me anymore.

**A WISE OWL UNDERSTANDS THAT JUST BECAUSE YOU
LIVE WITH SOMEONE DOESN'T MEAN YOU KNOW THEM.**

That evening, the entire campus was still abuzz with the
news of Eric Dalton's resignation. The second Dean
Marymount's email appeared in the inboxes of the student body, everyone had an opinion as to why Dalton was kicked
out, although Callie was pretty sure she knew the real reason:
clearly Brett had found out about Tinsley and Mr. Dalton.

Callie pushed open the door to the dining hall and was greeted
with the nauseating smell of refried beans. Mexican night.
Great. She put her hand on her stomach, as if she were trying to
reassure herself that it was still flat, and played with the collar
of her light purple cashmere Ya-Ya cowl-neck. Even if Tinsley
was suddenly her only real friend, she couldn't help but be
pleased for Brett. Hopefully neither she nor Tinsley would
smother the other in her sleep—that was all she needed.

"Can you believe it?" Callie whirled around to see Tinsley

looking unusually perturbed. She was fussing nervously with the pearl buttons at the neck of a silky teal Victorian-looking turtleneck. Her skin was almost completely covered up—so how come all the guys were still staring at her? She made Callie want to tear out her hair in jealousy.

"Sort of." Callie adjusted her charm bracelet. "Come on, you knew Brett would eventually fight back."

Tinsley gave Callie a withering glare, then smiled. "It was definitely Brett, then?"

"It had to be, right?" The two girls headed toward the food line. "Why else would he resign?" Callie snickered. "Unless he was afraid Tinsley Carmichael might be too much woman for him."

"He certainly didn't have any complaints in New York." Tinsley laughed.

"Have you talked to him?"

Tinsley picked up her tray. She would never have admitted it, but part of her excitement over Dalton came from the fact that she was stealing him from Brett. Once that was over, so was the rush of hooking up with him. She hadn't even thought about emailing him to see what was up—somehow, she didn't really care. It was already time for her to make her next move. "No."

"Are you going to?" Callie tapped her ragged nails against her plastic tray as they waited in the taco line. "Tacos. Gross."

Tinsley wrinkled her nose. "Looks like a salad night." She sauntered over to the salad bar. Callie followed. Tinsley still hadn't answered her. She looked distracted.

"There's something else you should know." Tinsley really couldn't imagine a worse time to tell Callie the bad news than in the dining hall, in front of the entire Waverly population, but she wanted her to know before they went back to their room tonight so she could be prepared. She pressed her red lips together.

"What?" Callie picked up a white plate, still warm from the dishwasher, on the other side of the salad bar and started to pile the freshly washed mesclun greens onto it.

Tinsley set down her tray. "I'm really sorry to be the one to tell you, but I didn't want you to find out from someone else." She took a deep breath, and Callie looked up at her in alarm, their eyes meeting across the clear plastic sneeze guard. "Jenny and Easy are totally together."

Callie paused mid-scoop. "What?" The temperature of her body immediately dropped twenty degrees. Her hands went clammy. She dropped the wooden fork back into the bin of greens. "That's not true."

Tinsley quickly picked up her tray and hurried over to Callie's side of the bar. She looked like she was about to faint. "I'm so sorry. But it is. I saw them in New York together."

"But that doesn't mean any . . ." Callie's voice faltered. Tinsley's pitying look could mean only one thing—it really was true. Easy liked Jenny? That *shrimp*? Those deformed-looking boobs? For real? Jenny had assured her—*promised* her—that nothing was going on! That *liar*! "How could she do that? We *live* together. I talk to her every fucking day! How could she not tell me?"

Tinsley touched Callie's arm. "She probably didn't want to piss you off."

"That bitch." Callie shivered and looked down to find herself holding her dinner fork in stabbing position. If Jenny wanted to live through the night, she might want to sleep somewhere else.

A WAVERLY OWL NEVER GOES INTO BATTLE
WITHOUT AN ALLY.

"Wait up!" Jenny spotted Brett leaving the library that night, her sleek red hair bouncing as she descended the steps. There was a definite spring to her step—her high-heeled lace-up Prada oxfords practically skipped across the sidewalk. She swung around to face Jenny and smiled.

"Hey." Brett flicked a lock of hair out of her eyes.

"It's nice to see you smiling." Jenny slipped the strap of her heavy suede bag across her body—it was too heavy to carry on one side, but she hated it when the strap cut between her breasts, calling even more attention to them than normal. Of course a backpack would be even worse.

Brett giggled. "I know I shouldn't be this happy, but I can't help it. It's just . . . poetic justice, you know. Even if Tinsley *is* going to kill me." The thought of sharing a room with Tinsley

now made her feel almost physically ill. Hard to believe that last
year they were giving each other manicures and gushing about
their most recent crushes. "I haven't seen her since the news broke."

They giggled as they walked back to the dorm. Inside, the
door to Dumbarton 303 was wide open, with "ABC" by the
Jackson Five blaring from the Callie's iPod docking station.
"Great," muttered Brett under her breath as she and Jenny drew
near. "They're having a disco party."

"Hey, Cal," Brett greeted Callie as she walked through the
doorway.

"Hello." Callie nodded, pulling on her pajamas. Strands of
her strawberry-blond hair stood straight up from the static. She
flopped down on her unmade bed.

"Sounds like you're in a great mood," Brett said, dropping
her antique Prada shopping tote to the floor carelessly.

Callie didn't respond. She slid the hair band she kept on her
wrist around a ponytail and fiddled with the volume on her
iPod. The music switched to a moody Belle & Sebastian song.

"I *love* this song," Jenny offered. Callie looked up, her hazel
eyes focused and cold, and clicked off the music. Suddenly the
silence in the room was deafening. Whoa.

"Well, look who it is," a new voice said, and all three of the
girls turned their heads to see Tinsley, in her Egyptian cotton
bathrobe, playing with the cap of a bottle of Evian. "Callie and
I wanted to talk to you both about something. We just wanted
to tell you both that you can't be in Café Society anymore."

Jenny's reddened face turned even redder. She glanced at

Brett. Why was Tinsley doing this? It seemed like an open declaration of war.

Brett's eyebrows scrunched together threateningly. "Oh, yeah?" She picked up her Brine field hockey stick as if she were preparing to whack Tinsley's head with it. "Is this because of Eric?"

Tinsley leaned her head against the door frame. "Eric?" she asked casually. She pretended to think about it. "Actually, yes, I'm kind of annoyed you got him fired just when we were starting to get close."

"How can you even say that with a straight face?" Brett demanded. "Who do you think you *are*?"

"I wouldn't be asking that question if I were you." Tinsley strode across the room and dropped the water bottle onto her bedside table before looking back at Brett. "*I know who I am.* Do you?"

Jenny, who had been following the rapid exchange with horror, felt completely lost. What was Tinsley hinting at? Whatever it was, it shocked Brett into silence pretty quickly.

Brett turned her back on Tinsley. A Dorothy Parker quote suddenly came to her mind: *The woman speaks eighteen languages, and can't say "No" in any of them.* When she turned back, her face was more composed and her lips were steady. "I know I'm not a *slut.*" She returned Tinsley's nasty smile. "That's something."

"You should think about who you hang out with, then." Callie spoke up for the first time since Tinsley's arrival. She was staring straight at Jenny, and her fury suddenly made a lot more sense. Tinsley must have seen her with Easy in New York yesterday.

For a millisecond, Jenny thought maybe she could make things better by promising not to see Easy anymore. Maybe things could go back to the way they were the first night at the pizza parlor. She wanted desperately to get that feeling back— that feeling of belonging, of getting drunk with the cool girls, of having them like her. But the second passed. Who was she kidding? She'd never wanted to be with a boy so badly in her entire life as she wanted to be with Easy. She wouldn't trade him for all the Tinsley Carmichaels and Callie Vernons in the world.

Brett was about to come to Jenny's defense when Jenny surprised herself by doing it on her own. "I know why you're angry with me," she said softly. "And I'm sorry. I didn't mean for it to happen, but I should have been honest from the beginning."

Callie had none of Tinsley's abilities to control her anger elegantly. Instead, her normally picture-perfect skin became red and blotchy and her left eyelid started to twitch. She looked unbalanced. "You're a liar," she snarled.

"Don't you realize what a hypocrite you're being?" Brett railed at Callie. "You're mad at Jenny for getting together with Easy *after* you guys broke up while *she*"—Brett gestured toward Tinsley with the curved end of her stick—"started chasing down Eric while I was *still with him?*" She glared at Tinsley. "That's so . . . *shitty.*"

"Honey." Tinsley gave Brett a pitying look. "You were never with him."

"Fuck you!" Brett whirled back to Callie. "And fuck you too. You can have your stupid, self-absorbed Café Society and your stupid, fucked-up games." Brett shook her head. Her fiery red

hair looked wild but regal. "I have better things to do." With
that, she stalked out of the room, leaving silence in her wake.

Jenny glanced at Callie. Tinsley was an enormous bitch, but
she still felt like she owed Callie something. She'd lied to her,
after all. "I'm sorry," she repeated. "Maybe one day you'll
forgive me?"

Callie's eye twitched. Not bloody likely.

A CLEVER OWL KNOWS A KISS IS NEVER

JUST A KISS.

Thank God it was Friday. Jenny had looked for Easy all day on Thursday but hadn't been able to find him. She'd wanted to talk to him about Callie and getting kicked out of Café Society, but given how pissed off Callie was, she hadn't wanted to just run around campus asking everyone if they'd seen him. Easy was probably just spending his time with Credo, enjoying the glorious blue skies before they turned cold and gloomy. But it *was* a little strange that he was MIA. They'd had such an amazing time in New York, and they'd flirted all through class on Wednesday afternoon. Didn't he miss her?

Now it was Friday, which meant art class again. She slipped through the door and saw Easy pulling his pastels and pad of thick pastel paper from his supply shelf. She came up behind him and ran her hand across his shoulders. "Hey."

Easy raised his head. His enormous blue eyes looked

stressed but happy to see her. "Oh . . . hi." He gave a distracted smile.

"Are you all right?" Jenny glanced around for Mrs. Silver, who was going around the room, checking in with students.

"Yeah, I'm fine." Easy raised his eyes. "What's up?"

"Can I talk to you for a second?" Jenny smiled at Alison, who was just now pulling her sketchpad from her shelf next to Jenny's. She raised one of her sleek eyebrows toward Easy and nodded her dark, pigtailed head. Jenny felt a twinge of regret that she wouldn't get to hang out with her anymore, now that she'd been unceremoniously kicked out of Café Society. But did that have to mean her social life at Waverly was over?

"Here?" Easy looked dubious.

Jenny grabbed his arm, feeling another little thrill of excitement at touching him. "No, let's go to the kiln room."

Easy raised his eyebrows. "That sounds kind of sassy." Jenny giggled.

Jenny pulled him into the small room around the corner from the supply shelves. It was a dark room with a single window looking out over the Hudson. Two large kilns and three small ones took up most of the space, and the room smelled like clay and dust. Shelves of pottery in varying degrees of completion lined both walls. It was a romantic place, and it reminded Jenny of the sexy scene in *Ghost* where Patrick Swayze and Demi Moore get all wild with the clay on the potter's wheel. Mmmm. Jenny stepped close to Easy and looked up at him with longing.

Easy smiled down at her. "Is this what you wanted to talk about?"

That brought Jenny back to reality. "Um, no. I just wanted to say that I've been kicked out of Café Society." The words sounded so silly. "I guess I'm not going to Boston."

Easy didn't look very surprised. "Yeah?"

"Yeah." Jenny stared down at her black-and-white-plaid ballet flats. "So," she said nervously, "are you still going to go?"

Easy let out his breath, and Jenny looked up at him in alarm. For the first time, she began to think that maybe something was seriously wrong. Her palms started to sweat. Maybe he hadn't had fun in the city after all? "I'm not sure yet," he admitted.

"Did I . . . did I do something? To make you mad at me?" Jenny bit her lip nervously.

"I don't know." He turned away from her for a minute and played with a clay pot on the top shelf. He was being an asshole; he knew it. But his mind had latched onto that awful thing Tinsley had told him in the city—that Jenny was making out with another guy—and Heath's IM. He had to find out if it was true, and he hoped Jenny would forgive him if he was wrong. But he had to know. "Any chance you were making out with another guy? Like . . . Monday night?"

Jenny's mouth fell open. She could feel her cheeks turn crimson when she remembered the stupid pizza boy kiss. "Oh my God . . . there *was* this stupid thing that happened." She stared at her shoes again. "It was an initiation rite for Tinsley's society. We all sort of kissed this . . ."

"Wait a sec." Easy ran his hands through his hair. "How do you 'sort of kiss' someone?" His eyes were blazing. "Either you kiss someone or you don't."

"Easy, I'm sorry. I'm so sorry." Jenny's enormous brown eyes—the ones he'd trusted—brimmed with tears, but Easy was too angry to be moved. "I kissed him, but I didn't mean to. It was just a . . . a dumb thing. Like a game . . . I *had* to. And I . . . I didn't know if we were exactly together yet. . . ."

"You didn't *mean* to? Your lips just accidentally found their way onto some dude's mouth?" He shook his head in disbelief. "I can't believe this." Easy picked up an ugly, lopsided bowl and clutched his fingers around it. He had the urge to hurl it against the wall and watch it break into a million pieces. He reached for the doorknob.

"Where are you going?" Jenny cried. Her hands were fumbling with a loose thread at the bottom of her light pink sweater.

She looked so sweet and distraught that Easy almost changed his mind. His heart was so full of the feeling that he might be making a huge mistake, ending something that felt this big and this right before it even had a chance to really begin. But then he pictured some asshole's lips mashed against hers and her kissing back. He opened the door. "I have to get to class. I'm on probation, remember?"

Jenny nodded miserably. "But please, you have to understand. Can't we talk about . . ."

"I think we should probably not talk for a while." He glanced over his shoulder at her, hesitated one more time, then walked away.

To: CallieVernon@waverly.edu;
SageFrancis@waverly.edu;
CelineColista@waverly.edu;
BennyCunningham@waverly.edu;
AlisonQuentin@waverly.edu;
VerenaArneval@waverly.edu
From: TinsleyCarmichael@waverly.edu
Date: Friday, September 20, 8:09 p.m.
Subject: Puttin' on the Ritz

My darlings,

Tomorrow evening begins with cocktails at 6 sharp, suite 605, at the Boston Ritz. To feel at home in our elegant surroundings, the dress code is glam glam glam.

Don't forget a toothbrush and sexy jammies, if you plan on wearing any at all.

Our next victim: he talks about himself a lot, yes, but there's no one on earth more ready to have a good time than Mr. Heath Ferro. I expect us all to make out with him at least once throughout the night. Let's make him earn that "pony" reputation.

Conspiratorially yours,

T

OwlNet   Instant Message Inbox

CallieVernon: Ohmigod, Heath? Are you kidding? He's been
                           around the block so many times he even smells
                           dirty.

TinsleyCarmichael: Tsk, tsk. You know he's the sexiest guy left on
                           campus . . . unless you think Easy would be
                           interested in being the society's next project??

CallieVernon: Don't even start with me.

OwlNet

HeathFerro: What train u taking to Boostoon?

EasyWalsh: I'm riding up with Jeremiah from Lucius. 2 seater.

HeathFerro: Seat this mofo: the girls are gonna give it to me 2nite.

EasyWalsh: Congrats.

HeathFerro: Jealous much?

EasyWalsh: Dude, could you be any more of a girl?

HeathFerro: I could. But then I'd have to go screw myself.

EasyWalsh: U do that.

A GOOD OWL KNOWS

HOW TO PARTY.

By six o'clock, presidential suite 605 was party central. The girls had turned the polished mahogany dining room table into the bar, with bottles of wine ordered from room service and several bottles of vodka and tonic water. Enormous trays of foreign cheeses and crackers and other unidentifiable yet elegant hors d'oeuvres crowded the table. Tinsley's iPod and Bose SoundDock were perched on an end table near the television cabinet, and the TV was tuned to Turner Classic Movies and muted. Humphrey Bogart and Lauren Bacall bantered silently across the black-and-white screen.

Callie, wearing a red ABS empire waist chiffon dress with a crinkled, tiered skirt, freshly purchased from one of those tiny, overpriced upstairs boutiques on Newbury Street, had collapsed miserably into a maize-colored brushed suede armchair. The suite itself was stunning—the kind of hotel room that would have impressed even Callie's picky mother—but Callie couldn't enjoy it. She missed Brett, who was probably smoking cigarettes with that traitor Jenny right now and giggling about how they got out of coming to this silly party in Boston. Grrr. The thought of Jenny—and Jenny with Easy, *her* Easy—made her reach for her glass of chardonnay.

"It's almost time!" Sage Francis announced in a lilting, wine-tinged voice. If she was half drunk already, she'd be passed out on the floor by the time things really heated up, Callie thought bitterly. Sage eagerly approached the connecting door to suite 606, which Tinsley had insisted stay closed until exactly six.

A deep, booming knock came from the other side of the door. Sage jumped back, and the girls giggled.

"Go ahead," Tinsley agreed. "It's time." All the girls wore dresses except Tinsley, who had poured herself into a snug-fitting Theory black satin pantsuit. The tuxedo jacket was sleek and low-cut, and there was no room for anything underneath it. She looked like Angelina Jolie the year she wore a suit to the Oscars. "Don't forget who's next on our list, ladies."

"I bet he's the first one through the door." Celine Colista adjusted the fresh flowers in one of the half dozen vases scattered around the room and glared resentfully at Tinsley's outfit. She looked boring and traditional in her slinky black cocktail dress.

"Ladies, ladies, everywhere!" Heath Ferro boomed as he sauntered into the room, wearing a red silk smoking jacket and looking like Hugh Hefner. "That's what I like to see." He proceeded to make his rounds of the room, giving everyone a tasteful peck on the cheek and a chance to feel his silky jacket.

"Told you." Celine nudged Benny Cunningham in the waist.

"Don't you look debonair," Tinsley teased as Heath leaned over Callie and gave her a wet kiss on the cheek.

"Or sleazy." Callie almost jumped at the sound of the familiar, drawling voice. Easy had walked into the room, wearing his Hives T-shirt and the pair of cuffed gray Ben Sherman trousers that he only wore when he had to look dressy. A black fedora was perched crookedly on his head. Her heart started to beat faster. Since they'd kicked Jenny and Brett out of Café Society, Callie had assumed Easy would stay behind with Jenny this weekend. She pretended to be angry with him, but God, all she wanted was to have him kiss her again like he used to.

Heath draped his arm around Easy's lean shoulders and planted a wet kiss on his cheek. "Don't be jealous, brother. There's plenty of love to go around." Heath grabbed Easy's fedora and plunked it down on Tinsley's head.

So why *was* Easy here and not snuggling up with Jenny in one of the empty dorm rooms? Was there trouble in paradise already? Callie was suddenly *much* more interested in the party. She decided to refill her drink.

"Surprised to see you here." Callie set her wineglass down on the mahogany table as Easy poured himself a stiff vodka tonic.

"Why's that?" Easy popped a lime slice into his drink and took a long swig.

"You know." Callie paused suggestively and waited until he turned to look at her before continuing. "Thought you were on probation."

"Oh." Easy scratched behind his left ear, something he always did when he didn't want to talk about something. Callie had to force herself to calm down. Just because he looked distracted didn't necessarily mean things were over with Jenny. "Whatever. Now that Dalton's out of there, I don't really have to watch my back."

But still . . . if he liked her that much, wouldn't he be with her right now and not two hundred miles away, in a hotel room full of beautifully dressed, drunken girls?

Callie moved a little closer to him. "Funny how that happened, isn't it? I mean, Dalton just suddenly resigns one day." Callie flicked her hair over her shoulder, trying to give Easy a good view of her long neck, which used to be one of his favorite parts of her.

Easy smiled down on her, and she felt like she had just swallowed some hot chocolate spiked with kahlua, the way it warmed her body up from the inside. "I know nothing." He raised his eyebrows mysteriously.

"I'm just glad you're here." Callie placed her hand on Easy's bare forearm, and she felt the tingles surging from her fingertips.

Easy stared at her hand. "What are you doing?"

"What?" Callie snatched her hand away and Easy stalked out to the balcony, where Jeremiah and Benny were smoking.

Callie felt a hand on her waist. "You look like a goddess." She whirled around, her hair flying into Brandon's eyes. He didn't seem to mind. In his Italian wool Theory pinstripe pants and black Hugo Boss French-cuffed button-down, he looked exactly like he always did—sophisticated, attractive, and completely boring. "Like Aphrodite. The goddess of love."

"Uh, thanks." Callie looked up as someone changed the music to dance tunes. She poured herself another glass of wine.

"Whenever you want a break from this, we can go back to the room I booked. For us."

"Brandon." Callie rubbed her hands across her face, threatening to mess up her makeup. But God, what was Brandon's deal? Did he really think she was going to leave the party to go back to his empty room and snuggle? Ever since she'd kissed him last week, he was acting like they were back together. She glanced around for Easy. "We're at a party. Act like it."

"Can you blame me for wanting to be alone with you? You look so gorgeous. I just want to . . . be near you." Okay, that was sweet. Callie felt a teeny bit better, but not enough to *leave* with him.

"Can't blame you for trying." Callie patted his face. "But stop."

"You guys look like an old married couple." Alan St. Girard came up and drooped an arm around each of them. Alan puckered his lips at Callie. "Got any lovin' for me?"

"Honey . . . ," Brandon started.

Honey? "I am *not* your honey, Brandon Buchanan." She waved her wineglass at him. "I am *nobody's* honey, all right?" She glared at him, suddenly furious that the only one who loved her was boring, predictable Brandon. She'd show him. She was *anything* but boring.

32

A WAVERLY OWL LEAVES NO DRUNKEN FRIEND
BEHIND—ESPECIALLY WITH HER CELL PHONE.

"Doesn't it seem so mellow without Tinsley and Callie around? I can feel my blood pressure lowering as I speak." Brett stretched out her long legs across the arm of the couch in Dumbarton's upstairs lounge. With all the girls in Café Society out for the night, the whole dorm felt quieter. She wore a lime green cap-sleeve tee with a pair of wide-leg black pants. On her lap was a plastic bowl filled with buttered microwave popcorn, freshly popped and slightly burned.

Jenny opened one of the dormer windows and waved out some of the burnt popcorn smoke. "I know what you mean." She breathed in the cold night air, letting it sting her lungs. "The two of them—they sort of make me forget how much I like it here."

"Yeah. Just tonight, walking across the quad and looking up and seeing all those stars . . . I mean, the sky doesn't look like that in New Jersey." Brett pulled the bottle of Stoli from her red leather Sigerson Morrison bag. It was already half empty. She poured some more into her mug of cranberry juice. "Need a refill?"

"Thanks." Jenny handed over her mug. Brett was from New Jersey? She'd gotten the impression that she was from East Hampton or else Nova Scotia or something. "I really love it here. It makes me feel so—I don't know—wholesome." It sounded moronic, but it was true. Waverly, with its groomed athletic fields and state-of-the-art libraries and art studios, its blue-blood student population with their perfect patrician noses and cashmere sweater vests, was strangely like some sort of earthly paradise. And while she'd felt a little awkward at times, something told her she belonged here.

Brett grinned. "Yeah, it's probably all the drinking and pot and sex going on that gives you that impression." She pulled a strand of bright red hair in front of her eyes and expertly scanned it for split ends. "But I know what you mean. I love it too." Her eyes clouded over a little. "Think how perfect it would be if Tinsley hadn't come back."

Jenny didn't even want to let herself think about that. Yes, it would be heavenly if Tinsley could just evaporate into thin air, if she'd run off with some rich international businessman she met in the halls of the Ritz-Bradley. "It feels like she's out to get us both."

"Probably because she is." Brett sat up and set the bowl of popcorn on the table. "But you know, fuck her. Fuck all those other girls. What are they doing right now? Getting shitfaced. Heath's probably running around buck-naked, trying to grope everyone."

Jenny cringed at that unpleasant image. Suddenly she was completely relieved she wasn't there in Boston, with Tinsley and Callie and the other girls. She was happy to be *here,* eating popcorn with Brett and gossiping. If only Easy weren't in Boston. If only Easy weren't furious with her. "I miss Easy."

Brett popped open the tab of a Diet Coke. "I know. I miss Jeremiah too." Ever since that day in the cemetery, she'd been thinking about him a lot. She wondered if he was seeing anyone at St. Lucius yet—he hadn't mentioned any other girls, but it was hard to believe that he could stay single for very long. He was the star of their football team and was sexy in a slightly goofy, natural way that endeared him to all members of the opposite sex. An image of him in his Gap boxers came to her, and she could almost feel her hand running along his sculpted stomach muscles. Mmmm. "Maybe I shouldn't have broken up with him."

"Really?" Jenny liked the idea of Brett with a boyfriend who wasn't a teacher, and Jeremiah was hot. "He sounds really sweet when you talk about him."

Brett groaned and took a handful of popcorn. "He *is* really sweet. I don't know what I was thinking—the whole Eric thing was fucked up." Brett popped a piece of singed popcorn into her mouth and chewed thoughtfully. "I guess it made me feel special to have someone like Eric take an interest in someone like me. He's practically, you know, a Rockefeller. . . ."

"What's that supposed to mean, someone like you? Of *course* he was interested in you." It was hard for Jenny to imagine someone as gorgeous as Brett, and as smart and funny, having any self-esteem problems. They were reserved for people like herself!

Brett sighed and took a long swig from her mug before leaning her head back on the couch. "Yeah, well, if you knew my whole story, you might not think that."

Jenny's eyes widened. "What are you talking about? You didn't, like, murder someone, did you?"

"No, it's nothing like that. It's just that I, sort of, have this totally embarrassing family." Brett pulled a strand of her hair in front of her eyes again and stared at it, like she was trying to avoid looking at Jenny. "And I can't help it—I'm just, you know, ashamed of it. But somehow I was able to talk to Eric about it, and he made me feel like it was no big deal at all. He almost seemed to like me even more because of it."

"Well, maybe I should have told you about my father earlier because that would totally have made you feel better." Jenny sank onto the couch next to Brett and placed her feet on the low, glass-topped coffee table. Not the brightest idea for a dorm— Jenny could easily imagine herself tripping over it after a few more drinks. "He once showed up for this awards ceremony at my school wearing a T-shirt under his blazer because all of his button-downs were wrinkled. Not so bad, you say? Maybe even kind of cool? Well, he wore a *tie* with it. With his IMPEACH NIXON *T-shirt*." Jenny hung her head but had to giggle at the memory. "Parents came up to me afterward and actually asked if my father was homeless. Seriously. Beat *that*."

Brett almost snorted with laughter. "I'm so sorry." She had to take deep breaths to keep her composure. "All right, well, at my eighth-grade graduation, my father actually handed out his business cards with coupons for ten percent off any collagen injections or nose jobs—to my *friends*. And my mother? She wore a pair of zebra-print boots she'd had especially made for her in Brazil, and everyone could totally see her thong." She could imagine the splash those boots would make at Waverly, where all the moms wore Ralph Lauren, Chanel, and Marni.

"But parents are totally *supposed* to be embarrassing, right? Otherwise they wouldn't be parents," Jenny said logically.

"I guess. . . . I just feel funny, being this sort of nouveau riche Jersey girl, here among all these old-money debutantes like Tinsley and Callie and Benny, you know?"

Suddenly, after getting the words out, Brett felt ten thousand pounds lighter. It was like she'd felt after telling Eric: relief. So, maybe it wasn't Eric who had made her feel that way at all—maybe it was herself? Brett swung her legs onto Jenny's lap, her mind going back to Jeremiah. "You know, when I talked to Jeremiah, it was like he wasn't even angry with me. Just sorry I'd been hurt."

"Why don't you call him?" Jenny suggested. "Maybe it would help if you could just hear the sound of his voice?" Something about vodka made her sentimental—it was like when she was PMSing, and if she even *thought* about *Edward Scissorhands*, her eyes would tear up. But with vodka, her feelings weren't always sad, just intense. Like right now, thinking of Easy, she could almost conjure up the smell of him.

"Nah. He's busy partying. I don't want to bug him." Brett poured the last trickle of cranberry juice into her mug. "Besides,

I broke up with him. I can't just run back to him the second I change my mind." Her lips formed a delicate pout.

"Do we have another bottle of cranberry juice in the room? I thought I saw one," Jenny asked absently, an idea slowly forming in her vodka-tinged brain.

"All right, lazybones. I'll go get it." Brett swung her legs to the floor a little sloppily and heaved herself onto her feet. "I wanted to get a sweater anyway."

As soon as Brett left the room, Jenny grabbed her friend's silver Nokia and scrolled through it for Jeremiah's number. Her heart was pounding in her ears, and she knew Brett would be furious with her, but what kind of friend would she be if she wasn't willing to risk pissing Brett off for her own good?

Jeremiah's voice mail picked up after only two rings, and Jenny almost forgot what she was going to say. "Hi, uh, Jeremiah. This is, um, Jenny, a friend of Brett's. I'm sorry to call you—I really hope I'm not bothering you. But I just wanted to let you know that Brett's been thinking about you, like, all the time, and she knows she made a huge mistake and she wants to ask you to forgive her, but she's too afraid to. I mean, she's totally in love with you, and I totally know because . . ." Jenny took a giant gulp of air. Was she making any sense at all? "Because I'm in love with someone too. And so I know what it looks like, and she's got it bad . . . And people who are in love really shouldn't let misunderstandings come between them."

Brett came back into the room to find Jenny using her phone. "What are you doing?" she shrieked, dropping the plastic liter bottle of cranberry juice and grabbing at the phone. "Are you crazy?"

Jenny danced away from Brett and tried to hurriedly finish the call. "So, all I'm saying is that you shouldn't let unimportant things get in the way of you being happy. Really. So, um, I'm going to go because Brett's going to kill me. But nice talking to you." She clicked off the phone and tossed it to Brett, who was just standing there with a horrified expression on her face.

"I can't believe you did that!"

"Are you going to kill me?"

Brett thought about it. "Who would I have to talk to then?" A slow, sheepish grin spread across her pretty face. "I just can't *believe* you did that!"

Jenny smiled, proud that she'd taken the initiative. If Brett was so bent out of shape over Jeremiah, it meant she belonged with him, right? And if she felt the same way about Easy, it meant they belonged together too. Right? She blew Brett a kiss. "Maybe you'll return the favor one day."

A SAVVY OWL KNOWS HOW TO
(RE)START THE PARTY.

After a few joints were passed around out on the balcony, the party took a turn toward the lethargic. Sleepy, satisfied bodies were draped in various states of repose across the expensive furniture. "Why does everyone have to act like a zombie after they smoke?" Tinsley demanded of Easy, who was slouched in a corner of the couch, lifelessly flicking through the cable channels. She tapped the toe of her Kate Spade satin-toed espadrille against Easy's shin. She could feel the ribbon ties around her calf slowly loosening. "Hello?"

"Why don't you do something to liven up the party for us, Tin?" Heath came up behind Tinsley and wrapped his arms around her. His whiskey breath stung her nose.

"That sounds like a dare." Tinsley flicked Heath's arms off her and strode across the room. If anyone loved a dare, she did.

First, off with the television. Tinsley poked the power button and *South Park* disappeared. Then she twirled the volume dial on the stereo and the new Black Eyed Peas song flooded the room. She narrowed her eyes as she watched everyone watching her— *this* was what she was waiting for. In one smooth motion, she hopped up onto the tall, mahogany desk against the wall of the living room. A large, gilded mirror hung behind it, and everyone stared as both Tinsley and her image started to swing her hips in sync to the heavy, pulsing beat. She fingered the plunging neckline of her jacket, her hand slowing as she neared the top button. Her thumb pushed it through the buttonhole.

Tinsley grinned. Suddenly it was a party again.

"Take it off!" Ryan Reynolds cried out drunkenly, leaping up from the armchair he was sharing with Celine while trying to slide his hands up her teal Betsey Johnson skirt. Celine glared at him. He didn't notice.

Tinsley smiled devilishly and tossed her long mane of wavy black hair. With excruciating slowness, she played with the second button, torturing her captive audience as long as she could before sliding it through its buttonhole. Her violet eyes stared down Heath across the room, and he lifted his head from Sage Francis's lap, where she'd been massaging his scalp. He clapped and hooted as Tinsley suddenly pulled her jacket down to reveal one bare shoulder.

Callie poured herself another glass of wine at the bar, irritated by Tinsley's antics. Did she always have to be the center of everything? She took a big gulp and looked around for Easy—she couldn't help it; she'd been doing it all night. Watching him out of the corner of her eye, counting how many girls he was talking to. It was pathetic, and she knew it.

But when she saw his eyes tracing the movements of Tinsley's body, she'd had enough.

"Help me up," Callie demanded as she slipped off her jeweled T-strap Jimmy Choos and took Tinsley's hand. "Oof."

"You're killing me!" Alan crawled on his knees over to the desk and bowed several times to the two girls, as if they were some sacred altar.

"Hey, baby." Tinsley pushed Callie's hair back behind her ear and whispered in it, "Work it." Tinsley stepped back and casually slid her jacket off to her elbows, revealing a sheer black La Perla bra, with strategically placed lacy embroidery to keep it from being entirely see-through. She tossed back her head and gave a throaty laugh that seemed to say she was perfectly comfortable dirty dancing on top of a bureau at the Ritz with her top off.

Callie wanted—no, *needed*—to be that carefree. And so it seemed like a good idea to slip first one spaghetti strap, then the other, off her shoulders and start to shimmy out of her red slip dress. She glanced at Easy, but he was no longer on the couch. In fact, he wasn't even in the room. What did she have to *do* to get his attention, damn it!

"What are you doing?" A face separated itself from the crowd. Brandon. He reached up to pull Callie down. She danced backward, out of his reach.

"I'm dancing, Brandon." She put her arm around Tinsley's waist, and the two of them moved their hips together. Maybe Easy would walk back in?

Heath, wearing Easy's fedora and a white terry-cloth Ritz-Bradley robe, came up behind Brandon and tried to pull him away. "Dude, you're ruining a good thing."

Brandon pushed him away. "You're drunk, Callie. Please, just . . . just come to our room."

"Brandon!" Callie shrieked, whirling around so fast she almost slid off the desk. "It's *your* room, not *our* room. Why don't you just go watch a gay porno on pay-per-view or something?" She glared at him before turning back to Tinsley, still dancing with a smirk on her face. "At least Heath is fun," she whispered to Tinsley, loud enough for Brandon to hear.

"Fine. Make a fool of yourself." Brandon shoved Heath away from him and stomped out the door. It looked like he was going to have more champagne and more chocolate-covered strawberries for himself.

A WISE OWL UNDERSTANDS THAT A DRUNKEN
MESSAGE IS OFTEN THE MOST SINCERE.

"Walsh." Jeremiah grabbed Easy's arm as it reached for the almost-empty bottle of Jack Daniels. "You'd better slow down. You are *wrecked.*"

Easy had stumbled over to the makeshift bar as soon as the girls had hopped onto the desk. Sure, he enjoyed a good show as much as anyone else, but ever since realizing Tinsley had tried to get him kicked out of Waverly, everything about her seemed so *calculated.* Yeah, she was gorgeous and exotic and exciting, but she was also a giant bitch. And Easy didn't have time for that. Besides, the way Callie fell all over herself trying to keep up with Tinsley made him a little sick. Why'd she even give a shit about what other people thought of her? That was one of the things about Callie that had always driven him insane. "Thanks, bro, but I'm good." The bottle clanked against his glass, and the rest of the liquid splashed against his melting ice cubes.

"I've got something that'll make you feel even better."
Jeremiah had a weird smile on his face, like he'd just discovered Keira Knightley naked in one of the suite's many closets.

"I don't really want to smoke, dude." Easy had dragged himself to Boston even though he wasn't in a partying mood. All
he'd wanted to do tonight was bring a couple of blankets out to
the clearing in the woods and curl up with Jenny, watching the
stars. But he was too proud to stay home from Boston after what
Jenny had done.

"No weed." Jeremiah pulled his black Motorola from the
pocket of his Diesel jeans. "I just got this really sexy message on
my voice mail about how much Brett is in love with me."

"That's awesome, dude." Easy threw back his glass of rum.
"Good for you."

"No, good for *you* too." Jeremiah patted Easy on the back. "It
was from that girl, Jenny. And she said some other pretty interesting stuff too. You've got to listen." He punched some num-
bers into his phone and handed it to Easy.

Easy held it to his ear and let Jenny's warm, slightly drunk
voice sweep over him like the best kind of drug. "Because I'm in
love with someone too," he heard her say, and suddenly his anger
disappeared. All he wanted was to be holding her as she was
saying that.

"Hot, isn't it?" Jeremiah nudged Easy in the ribs.

Easy stared at the brocade wallpaper in a daze. What was he doing
here, at the stupid Ritz in Boston? He wasn't interested in watching
Heath Ferro get naked with the girls. The only girl he wanted to
get naked with was back at Waverly. "Are you okay to drive?"

Jeremiah grinned. "Great minds think alike." He patted the pocket of his velvet blazer, and his keys clinked inside. "I wasn't drinking tonight. Are you ready to get the hell outta here?"

"I'm already gone."

35

A WAVERLY OWL SHOULD AT LEAST GIVE THE IMPRESSION OF TRYING TO FOLLOW THE RULES.

Callie awoke with a start. She'd fallen into a drunken half sleep and had one of those intense dreams that was so vivid, so exact that it felt completely real. She was lying beneath her double-cashmere blanket with Easy, both of them in their underwear, and his fingertips were running up and down her bare stomach, sending chills down her spine. He smelled exactly like he always smelled, like horses and hay and cigarettes, and when he kissed her, Callie could swear his lips were actually on hers at that very moment.

Except it wasn't Easy kissing her. It was Heath Ferro. "Wake up, sleeping beauty."

Callie pulled away from him and wiped the back of her hand across her mouth. Tears almost sprang to her eyes when she realized Easy wasn't here and that they weren't in her bed. Her half-dressed body was splayed against the velvety hotel couch.

The coffee table in front of her was cluttered with empty wine-glasses and crumpled napkins. A pair of heather gray Ralph Lauren boxer briefs were crumpled on the table. Someone on the couch was braiding her hair. She looked up. Tinsley.

"Don't pass out again." Callie surveyed the room. No one else was even awake or, at least, moving. Benny Cunningham was lying facedown on the Oriental rug, her skirt pulled up to reveal her red Calvin Klein thong. She'd be mortified if she were conscious. For a moment, Callie thought about taking a photo with her camera phone, but she had no idea where she'd left it. And besides, Heath now had his tongue in her ear.

"Get off me, Heath." Callie tried to stand up, but her legs weren't working correctly and she sank back to the floor.

"You've already forgotten the rule?" Heath asked drowsily. "It's be-nice-to-Heath time."

"Come on." Tinsley climbed onto Heath's lap. "He's the only one who made it through our party conscious. We have to reward him."

"Oh, yes, yes." Heath sighed. "Reward me. Please."

Callie grabbed at one of the glasses that still had an inch of wine in it. She swallowed it quickly. What would her mother think if she saw her now, drinking someone else's probably back-washed glass of wine, about to hook up with the sluttiest guy at Waverly in a trashed suite at the Boston Ritz? She'd have a heart attack. That almost made it all bearable.

Tinsley giggled and slowly rose from Heath's lap. She shook out her mane of dark hair and looked impatiently down at him.

"Let's go out on the balcony," Heath suggested, a wicked,

drunken grin on his lips. "The sun's going to come up soon. You can see it rise over Boston Harbor." On his way toward the sliding glass door, he grabbed the velour blanket that was covering the bodies of Ryan and Alison on the floor. They were both snoring. "We might need this."

"We won't need *this*," Tinsley said as she slid the bathrobe off her shoulders and scampered over to the door, wearing only her bra and panties. She dropped it over the still-sleeping Ryan and Alison. "Actually, I think the balcony is a no-clothing-allowed area, so if you're coming, you'd better change." She grinned at Callie pointedly.

Callie quickly swallowed some more wine. Let Tinsley show her up? Not this time. What did she care, anyway? Easy was nowhere in sight and hadn't been for the past few hours, what little Callie could remember of them. She felt completely lost, like everything in the entire world was upside down, and so who cared if she made one more giant mistake? It was almost soothing to know she was taking an active part in destroying her own life instead of just letting it happen.

"Meet you out there." With that, she pulled her red dress over her head and walked out to the balcony, not about to let Tinsley win. At least, not this time.

SOMETIMES AN OWL MUST AWAKEN
IN ORDER TO DREAM.

Jenny opened her eyes at the sound of voices. She'd been having a nightmare, one of those awful ones where you got all the way to class before realizing that you were completely naked. In the dream, everyone in the classroom— Mr. Wilde's AP American History classroom—was coming up to Jenny and poking at her and trying to give her messy, wet kisses. Only Easy, sitting by himself at a desk in the corner, wasn't paying attention to her. He was drawing a picture of a beautiful girl—when Jenny squinted to get a better look, she saw it was Tinsley.

But now she was awake. And there were *definitely* voices. She blinked a few times, trying to get her eyes to adjust to the dark, and could make out a figure climbing into Brett's bed. A peal of giggles filled the dark room, and Jenny, still groggy with sleep and vodka, remembered the last time she'd been awakened in the middle of the night by a boy climbing into her roommate's bed. Her whole body remembered how Easy had ended up sitting on her bed, rubbing her back. Her stomach felt sick with longing.

What was going on? "Jeremiah!" she heard Brett whisper happily. "When did you guys get back?"

You *guys*? Jenny's heart started to beat faster as she tried to understand what was happening. Did that mean . . .

"Hey." Someone crouched down near Jenny's head. It was Easy.

"How did you . . ." Jenny shot up in bed, feeling a little too skimpily dressed in her black Calvin Klein tank and matching boy shorts. "What happened to the Ritz?"

Easy shifted his lanky body onto Jenny's bed. Was this really happening? Was she getting a second chance? He reached for her hair and tucked it behind her ear. "The Ritz is way overrated."

If Jenny was a cat, she would have purred. "Oh."

He cleared his throat. "Truth is, I realized it wasn't where I really wanted to be."

Jenny swallowed. Was her breath okay? Did she smell?

Easy grinned. "Come on, let's get out of here. I want to show you something."

Jenny tossed off her blankets and hopped out of bed, feeling Easy's eyes watching her body. Instead of feeling nervous, it just made her feel . . . warm. "Remember what happened last time you were in this room?"

"How could I forget?"

After pulling on the first pair of pants she found—her Miss

Sixty stretchy jeans—and her cinnamon-colored sweater coat from Anthropologie, Jenny let Easy grab her hand and lead her toward the door. She didn't ask where they were going—it didn't matter. Brett and Jeremiah, snuggled under Brett's thick down comforter, were in their own world.

"Are you cold?" Easy asked when the two of them were sitting on top of the bluffs, overlooking the slow-moving Hudson. The sky was lightening to a smoky gray, and Easy wanted to watch the sun rise. He put his arm around her shoulders.

"No." She leaned her head into Easy's neck, breathing in his smell.

One hand tightened around her, and his other one pulled a cigarette away from his mouth. He had lit it a few minutes ago, his fingers trembling a little. Like he was *nervous*, Jenny thought in amazement.

She looked up at him. "About that other stuff . . ."

Easy shook his head. "I overreacted." He took a drag from the cigarette and leaned back on the grass, looking straight up at the disappearing stars in the sky. "You were just having fun with your friends. It's okay."

"No." Jenny shook her head. She tugged at a lint ball forming on her sweater. "I mean, yeah. But . . . I would have been totally crushed if I'd heard about you, you know, kissing someone else." She sighed and felt herself wanting to be completely honest with Easy, even if it meant looking uncool or childish. "I just—wanted to belong, and I got swept up in doing what all the cool girls were doing."

"They've got nothing on you. Seriously."

Birds were starting to chirp, and it felt like the whole world was waking up, even though the sun still hadn't appeared over the horizon. She glanced up at Easy and took a deep breath. "I've never felt like this before."

Easy stubbed his cigarette into the dewy grass next to him and pulled Jenny down on top of him. His blue eyes looked almost black in the darkness. He nodded slowly and swallowed noisily like something was caught in his throat. "I know."

I know. That's all he needed to say. Jenny was so giddy she thought she might black out, so before she had the chance to, she kissed Easy the way she dreamed of kissing him all those other nights.

A PROUD OWL WILL NOT BE PRESSURED INTO
DOING THINGS SHE FINDS REPULSIVE.

Heath had pushed the two thickly padded chaise lounges on the balcony together to form a sort of regal outdoor bed. The streets below them were empty and lonely-looking, with only a few stray cars and cabs roaming around, their headlights still on in the gray early-morning air. It was chilly, and Callie felt weary and exhausted, but she wasn't about to head back inside for a nap. Instead, she curled under the velour blanket next to Heath, with Tinsley huddled on the other side of him.

Callie yawned and glanced at the other balconies on both sides of them—no one else seemed to think that a pre-dawn September morning was particularly romantic. She couldn't blame them. Heath finished his cigarette and tucked his hands under the blanket.

"Comfy, ladies?"

Tinsley, who had the blanket pulled up to her chin, slapped at one of Heath's hands that had strayed too far. "No," she admonished him sternly. "You can only go where I tell you." She reached for his hand beneath the blanket. "Like, here."

"Oh my God." Heath's eyes almost rolled back into his head. "I love this rule."

Jealously, Callie grabbed Heath's other hand. "Or here," she announced, pressing Heath's sweaty palm onto her collarbone.

"You're torturing me," Heath moaned, still with an ecstatic grin on his face. This was shaping up to be the best night of his life, Callie noted. Thank God, Callie had thought to kick his digital camera under the sofa—she didn't want any pictures of *this* surfacing in the Atlanta newspapers.

"How's this?" Tinsley's eyes flashed wickedly as she moved Heath's hand somewhere else.

Callie was about to do the same when she felt Heath's hand trying to slide its way down her body all on its own. Uh, *no!* Feeling his wiggling fingers was like a disgusting wake-up call—why the hell was she competing with Tinsley for *Heath Ferro?* Why was she letting herself be *groped* by him? She didn't even *like* him!

"Get off me, perv!" Callie pushed Heath's wandering hands away and jumped out from under the blanket into the chilly morning air, feeling instantly triumphant. She was tired of trying to impress Tinsley. It was *exhausting.*

For a minute, Callie forgot she was almost naked. Standing there, she felt her drunkenness slowly wear off as she gazed at the city of Boston. She felt almost queenly, goddesslike, as Brandon liked to tell her. She'd go inside, take a shower to wash off all traces of Heath's hands, put on some clean pajamas, and fall into a deep, relaxing sleep.

Her thoughts were interrupted by an explosion of sound as the door to the neighboring balcony slid open and the air suddenly filled with the familiar voices of *Good Morning America*. Before Callie could duck for cover, Dean Marymount stepped out, in a white fluffy robe exactly like the one Heath had been wearing earlier.

His eyes fixed on Callie, freezing her in place until a pair of vaguely familiar freckled arms wound around Marymount's waist. Angelica Pardee stepped outside, wearing a matching Ritz bathrobe.

"Callie!" She gasped in horror.

"Oh, *fuck*!" Callie cried, then slapped her hand to her mouth. Heath and Tinsley jumped up from the chaise, wrapped in the blanket, and turned to see what the problem was. Callie darted beneath the blanket. Dean Marymount had seen her underwear!

But that didn't seem like their biggest problem at the moment.

"This is a bit awkward," Dean Marymount admitted dryly, unable to hide the irritation in his voice.

"I'll say," Heath slurred.

"Wipe that smirk off your face, young man." Heath immediately stopped smiling. Marymount turned and whispered to Pardee, who disappeared inside. "Now, I don't know what you three are doing in Boston when you should be back in your beds at Waverly. And I don't want to know."

"Dean Marymount, I can explain." Tinsley's voice was innocent and persuasive, but even she knew that crouched there on the balcony at the Ritz, nearly naked beneath an overcrowded blanket, she had little to no credibility.

Marymount cut her off. "I'm sure you can. But I'm not interested." Strangely enough, he looked far more regal and intimidating in his bathrobe than he ever did in a suit. Even with his mussed-up, post-coital gray hair. Ew! "You are to get back to school. *Now.*" He glanced at his wrist before realizing he wasn't wearing a watch. "And no one will say a word—*about any of this.*" He stared at each of them individually, threatening them with just a glance. It was an impressive performance, Callie thought, considering he had just been caught messing around with someone else's wife.

But best to be humble, apologize, and get the hell back to Waverly. "Yes, sir." Tinsley hung her head. "We're very sorry, sir. We'll be on the next train" She couldn't risk getting expelled *again.*

Marymount almost shouted. "Get moving! If you're not back by nine A.M., I'll have to call your parents."

All three of them scrambled for the door in such a hurry that Heath didn't even notice Callie toss his pants off the balcony.

38

**A WAVERLY OWL KNOWS THAT SOMETIMES THE
SUBTLEST PUNISHMENTS CAN BE THE HARSHEST.**

Several minutes before nine, a silver Mercedes-Benz pulled
to a stop in front of the Waverly gate. The rear doors
opened, and three very disheveled owls tumbled out,
their long night of drinking and debauchery obvious to all.
Callie and Tinsley's faces were smeared with remnants of last
night's makeup.

"Run!" Tinsley ordered after tossing some large bills at the
driver and slamming the door shut. She'd called a car service
the second they'd gotten back inside the hotel room and left a
note for the others saying that they were going for a ride around
the city and would see them back at school. Callie couldn't think
about anything except the fact that Dean Marymount had seen
her practically naked. *Gross.* Thank God *he* hadn't been naked!

Heath took off, sprinting across campus with his black
leather John Varvatos overnight bag thudding against his hip.

Callie rolled her eyes as she and Tinsley jogged across the wet grass. "Loser."

"At least he makes things interesting." Tinsley paused for a moment to tug off her BCBG Max Azria satin wedges. She had to buy some more practical shoes. "Come on, Cal, speed it up. We've got, like, two minutes till nine."

Callie had stopped and was holding her hands to her stomach. It had been heaving the entire ride home, and now with the running, it was too much for it to handle. She leaned over one of the groomed flower beds and heaved.

"Shit." Tinsley measured the distance they still had to cover to their dorm—there's no way they were going to make it if they had to wait for Callie to finish puking. Fuck.

Callie wiped her mouth on the sleeve of her black Juicy Couture tie-front sweater. Of course this was how it would end—her alone, facedown in her own vomit on the Waverly lawn for the entire campus to see. She wanted to die. "You go ahead."

But Tinsley didn't move. Instead, she unzipped her Prada nylon tote bag and dug through it until she pulled out a half-full bottle of water. "Here." She handed it to Callie. "Drink."

Callie's eyes teared up. All right, so maybe Tinsley wasn't a complete bitch.

Ten minutes later, when they tiptoed into Dumbarton, they thought they were home free. Until, that is, they passed the door to the common room and saw Dean Marymount, leaning against the fireplace, waiting.

"You're late." He sighed, clearly still pissed. He ran a hand over his graying comb-over.

"Like, five minutes!" Callie cried, then clamped her mouth shut for fear of projectile vomiting all over him.

Tinsley spoke up pleadingly. "Come on, do you *have* to punish us?"

"Unfortunately, I do." Marymount straightened his maroon-and-navy tie—what was he doing wearing a tie on a Sunday morning, and how the hell had he gotten back to campus so quickly? "This institution has rules that must be upheld. However"—he looked at them pointedly—"because of extenuating circumstances, your punishment will be considerably lighter than it should be. Starting immediately, you two will no longer be allowed to live together. We've been able to do some rearranging, and a room on the first floor has opened up. Callie and Jenny Humphrey will remain in Dumbarton 303, while Tinsley and Brett Messerschmidt will move to Dumbarton 121."

Tinsley's mouth fell open. "You've *got* to be kidding me." She and Brett, alone? Talk about awkward. Maybe they could discuss Eric's kissing techniques while they lay in bed at night. She almost snickered, it was so absurd. And Callie and Jenny? They could compare notes on Easy while painting each other's toenails. Not. The administration really couldn't have planned a more perfect punishment for any of them.

Marymount gave her a sharp look. "The room is vacant now. It shouldn't take you too long to get resettled." He headed toward the door. "The sooner you get started, the better."

"That fucker!" Callie muttered fiercely the second the door closed behind him. She bit at her fingernail in frustration. "How can I be expected to live with that little *slut*? She'll probably sleep with Easy, like, every night."

"Kind of like you never did?" Tinsley blew Callie a kiss. Callie glared back at her, but Tinsley didn't care. She felt strangely excited about the whole situation. Life was too boring if things like this didn't happen every once in a while to shake it all up. "Come on, let's go break the news."

A WAVERLY OWL SHOULD BE OPTIMISTIC—
BUT NOT STUPID.

Twenty minutes later, Jenny's cell phone vibrated with an incoming call, jolting her awake. She had fallen asleep against Easy's chest as the two of them cuddled on the bluffs, wrapped in several thick, scratchy horse blankets. They'd been too busy kissing to pay much attention to the sunrise and had dozed off in the dreamy yellow-and-purple dawn. Jenny didn't care. She had a feeling there would be more sunrises with Easy in her future.

"Hello?" Jenny whispered, not wanting to awaken Easy, who was breathing softly.

"You are not going to believe this!" Brett was practically shrieking. Jenny sneaked out from under the blanket and took a few steps away from where Easy was still lying, her burgundy retro Campers sliding a little on the dewy grass. "Callie and Tinsley got caught in Boston. And guess what their punishment is?" Brett paused for half a second, not giving Jenny a chance to even guess. "They're *splitting them up.*"

"What do you mean, splitting them up?" Jenny asked, not comprehending. "How can they do that when we all . . ."

"They're making Tinsley move to a different room with *me*!" Brett was livid. "And you're with *Callie.*"

Jenny was suddenly wide awake. "Can they *do* that? That's so not fair!" Just when everything was starting to fall into place, Waverly was going to split up her and Brett because Tinsley and Callie had gotten caught? And leave her alone with Callie Vernon, who hated Jenny's guts so much she could probably stab a nail file into her heart while she was sleeping and not think twice about it? "It's not possible."

"Well, it's happening," Brett announced bitterly. "Tinsley just filled one of her Louis Vuitton bags with shoes and dragged it down the stairs. I'm supposed to start moving my stuff too. Where the hell are you, by the way?"

Jenny smiled for the first time since Brett had called. She glanced over her shoulder and saw Easy sitting up and stretching his long arms over his head, his hair sticking up in a million different directions. One cheek was covered with indentation marks from where he'd fallen asleep on the wool blanket. Jenny could feel the dew seeping into her sneakers and the warmth of the morning sun on her face. "I am exactly where I want to be right now."

"Good." She could hear Brett grinning through the phone. "Just come save me soon."

"Something wrong?" Easy's warm, sleepy voice murmured as Jenny hung up the phone. She felt her heartbeat quicken and crawled back under the horse blankets for one last long kiss. So Dean Marymount was messing up their living arrangements. How bad could it be?

OwlNet Instant Message Inbox

TinsleyCarmichael: I still can't believe it. Where r u?

CallieVernon: Waiting 4 Jenny to come out of hiding.

TinsleyCarmichael: God this is going to be fun!

CallieVernon: Ur crazy.

TinsleyCarmichael: Obviously.

CallieVernon: It's good to have you back T.

TinsleyCarmichael: And I'm just getting started...

FOUR BEST FRIENDS. FOUR HIGH SCHOOL DIPLOMAS.
ONE BOMBSHELL ANNOUNCEMENT THAT CHANGES EVERYTHING.

Harper Waddle, Sophie Bushell, and Kate Foster are about to commit
the ultimate suburban sin—bailing on college to pursue their dreams.
Middlebury-bound Becca Winsberg is convinced her friends have gone
insane...until they remind her she just might have a dream of her own.
So what if their lives are bass ackwards and belly up? They'll always have
each other.

BASS ACKWARDS AND BELLY UP

AVAILABLE NOW